TIME SPLIT BRIGGS

By Patricia Smith

Also by Patricia Smith

Time Split
Distant Suns
Distant Suns – The Journey Home
Distant Suns – The Silexous
Islands – The Epidemic
Nebathan

Prologue

Havelberg, Germany, 15th March 1930

Sarah suddenly found herself standing near a town square, the cry still deep in her throat. Her initial shock gave way instantly to surprise when she realised everything Jason had said was true. She had wanted to believe him but, despite this, a small part of her mind had denied it could ever be possible – yet here she was in Jason's Germany.

A demonstration was taking place and in the commotion, nobody had even noticed her unusual arrival.

Quickly she looked around. There was no time to lose. She had to find Jason; she had to find him *now*. Three minutes, her mind kept screaming, only three minutes, he had said.

She scanned the streets, her senses on high alert, but could not see him anywhere. She started towards the square, then suddenly she was bumped from behind. She glanced at the perpetrator, as they passed, and was shocked to see it was Jason.

She tried to grab him, but missed.

"Jason!" she yelled. "Stop! You must listen!"

He continued through the crowd, the noise of the demonstration drowning out her cries, oblivious to her presence.

Sarah could see the door to a building across the street open; some men in uniform were making their way down the stairs.

As Jason crossed the road towards them, she found herself caught up in the crowd. Pushing against the mass, she forced her way through the demonstrators and was just about to break free when her right arm was abruptly grabbed from behind.

She looked back, shocked, then stopped and stared, her mouth open in astonishment. For vital seconds it seemed as if time was no longer moving, but instead was frozen like ice. The crowd around her blurred as though part of a dream and the only reality was the man who stood before her. “Briggs,” she said. “How the hell did you get here?”

A flash of light snapped Sarah from her daze and she looked down in time to see the glint of a blade discreetly clutched near the soldier’s left hip. Shocked, she tried to pull back, but he held her in place so firmly she barely expanded the distance between them and was still comfortably within the man’s reach.

It immediately became apparent he was just toying with her when suddenly she found she was no longer moving away, but instead was being dragged closer.

“If you don’t struggle, I’ll make this quick,” he hissed, his face an emotionless mask.

Sarah screamed, aware she was in a square full of people. She did not expect Briggs to be phased, but still, the attention it would draw would be undesirable, especially if he was about to commit cold-blooded murder.

She knew the man was cool under pressure, but she hoped that this would be enough to force him to back down.

She felt him pause, just for a moment, and immediately took advantage of the hesitation. She pulled back again as hard as she could, writhing her body from side to side, to loosen his grip.

Briggs raised the knife when silencing the woman took priority over discretion. A successful blow just behind the ear would sever her spinal cord with minimum blood loss, terminating her life instantly. To the casual onlooker it would appear as though she had just fainted.

Sarah raised her free hand in a vain attempt to protect herself, then suddenly she was flung to the floor. She landed on her side. Briefly confused by the change of events, she was convinced at first she had been stabbed, but a quick check revealed no blood and she also realised there was no pain. She looked up from the ground and saw two men trying to wrestle the knife off Briggs.

For a moment, it seemed as though the young, powerful individuals may get the better of the soldier, who had been caught off guard by the assault, but his training and ruthlessness was not to be overpowered by mere youth.

A quick twist of the wrist loosened the grip of the man who had a hold of his knife hand and in a move so fast it was impossible to see it coming, Briggs punched him on the side of the jaw, using the weapon to add weight to his blow. As the young man crumpled to the floor, knocked out cold, Briggs turned his attention to his colleague, who had been trying to wrestle the soldier from behind.

Reversing the movement, he swung the knife in a clockwise direction and plunged the blade deep into the man's neck.

Behind Briggs a look of shock briefly washed over the German's face before he loosened his grip, dropped to his knees and fell forward to lie diagonal to his colleague.

Sarah scrambled backwards, distancing herself from the scene, before climbing to her feet, desperate to escape Briggs, but more importantly, to stop Jason. She pushed through the crowd and broke clear just in time to see the scientist, gun in hand, stepping backwards away from the guards.

"Jason! Stop!" she screamed, then jumped when the sound of gunfire echoed off the buildings surrounding the square.

She turned her back on the drama as first the guard and then the official, who had been standing behind him for protection, fell to the ground.

Briggs cleared the crowd, he stopped – and for a heartbeat, stood staring smugly at Sarah. He had not killed her, but had still achieved the desired outcome. The altered timeline was saved; Hitler was as good as dead. He blinked and then she was gone.

Chapter One

Nuclear Bunker, Kenton Bankfoot, Newcastle-upon-Tyne

Sarah winced, then covered her eyes when the world around her suddenly became startlingly, painfully bright.

She was thrust over six weeks ago into a post-nuclear world where all sources of mains electricity had been fried in the massive electromagnetic pulse emitted by the nuclear bomb at the point of detonation. Since then the only source of light by night had been fire and by day the sun, softened by a haze of dust, which appeared at first to be the precursor of a nuclear winter.

A month of snow, darkened with the ash of thousands of bodies combined with the residue blasted from the buildings and ground from the nearby city of Newcastle-upon-Tyne, vaporised in the glare of the small sun, helped scrub the sky clean.

As a result of living in the gloom of the day and near blackness of night, Sarah had become unaccustomed to the harsh unforgiving brightness of strip lighting.

She cracked a gap in her fingers to risk a peek and found she was standing in an identical teleporter to the one she had entered in the basement in Ponteland just five minutes ago. She lowered her hands, blinking rapidly at first until her eyes gradually adjusted to the glare, and looked around.

She was in a windowless room about four metres square. Six rows of empty shelves lined the wall ahead. On her left there was a door and on her right was a table and chair, the only other furniture in the room apart from the machine.

She opened the door to the teleporter and stepped out. The room was very clinical-looking with white washed concrete walls and a plain cream tiled floor.

She crossed to the table, a very basic, plywood design, stained with cup rings and cigarette burns, which was devised to be functional rather than visually pleasing, as was the chair, which was made from untreated, bare pine.

The only other object in the room, an A4-sized bound report, sat in the centre of the desk.

The cover of the document was a plain heavy-duty off-white card and it was bound with a thick red weave. '*Top Secret*' was written in large letters across the front.

At one time that would have been enough to deter Sarah from opening the report, but that was before she had to fight for her life to survive a nuclear apocalypse. Now, she knew any advantage had to be utilised and some advantages were disguised as simple books, a fact she discovered when she found 'The Essential Guide to Surviving in the Wild' in a small shop at the top of Morpeth High Street.

She lifted the corner of the cover and gently pulled the document open. It fell away as if it had been well-read and stayed wide in the 10 o'clock position. The first page gave more information about the document.

'*Report on the Time Displacement Unit and Its Consequences by Jason Hudson.*'

Sarah inhaled sharply. She flicked past the contents page and for the next five minutes scanned the report, which outlined the transition from a teleporter to a time travel device once the introduction of live matter occurred. It also contained schematics and instructions on the machine's implementation and described the horrific consequences of its use. The final pages of the document detailed Jason's experiences in the altered timeline, his encounter with Sarah and Briggs, along with a recommendation to dismantle the machine and to destroy the notes.

Slowly, she closed the booklet. It was now obvious that the device and report had somehow come into Briggs' possession, but how?

She turned to face the door. She knew if she had returned to this machine, then at some point, potentially soon, Briggs would also come back to the same location. Still, despite the danger she had to know what lay beyond this room; not just the room, but more precisely what was happening outside.

She stepped up to the door. She was shocked to find, on closer inspection, it was made of metal. It appeared to have been designed for fortification, which she found surprising on an internal structure, and was surrounded by a snug metal frame which overlapped the barrier to provide additional protection.

She flicked the light switch off, plunging the room into darkness, before carefully groping for the handle and slowly lowering it down.

The door was heavier than she anticipated and she had to lean forward to gain enough leverage to get it initially moving. As it began to open, light bled into the room when a gap appeared between the structures. She paused, listening for any sounds of movement or any other signs of activity. When she was happy all seemed quiet, she risked opening it further until it was wide enough for her to peer outside.

A dimly lit corridor lined with pipes and cabling travelled for some distance ahead. At the far end Sarah could see another door shrouded in near darkness. The gentle hum of a motor, at a distant location, was the only sound to be heard droning beyond the room.

She opened the door fully and stepped cautiously out into the corridor, then controlling the swing, held the barrier until it settled back into its housing.

She turned and made her way down the passage. As she prowled the length, as quietly as she could, her muscles ached on multiple levels. She was still sore from the beating she took in the basement from Andrews, Briggs' second-in-command, less than twenty-four hours ago. Poor food and radiation poisoning had also taken their toll on her general health and to top it all, the tightness of her body, poised ready to spring back to the room at a moment's notice, put a further strain on her already fragile frame.

As she moved further into the passage, Sarah noticed a door on the left, previously unseen from the far end. As she drew closer, she saw it was another heavy-duty, reinforced barrier like the one she had just left behind.

She stopped and again paused to listen for sounds before slowly turning the handle and peering into the room. Complete blackness, with such depth it was obvious even the faintest source of light was unavailable, greeted her. She reached around and groped at the wall briefly before finding a switch and turning it on.

Energy-efficient, low power lights glowed dimly at first, but quickly brightened enough for her to soon take in her surroundings.

The room opened out into a substantial area which appeared to be living quarters. Several couches encircling three separate large square low coffee tables gave the impression the complex was designed to comfortably house more than just a few people. The same could be said for a long wall on the left adorned with a floor-to-ceiling bookshelf, fitted with a ladder attached to runners for easy access, which was completely crammed with a wide variety of books.

Directly ahead a door stood open, but again the room was in darkness. Still, enough light from the lounge area leaked into the opening for Sarah to see that it looked like a kitchen. Easy clean steel benches topped metal cupboards near the door, but the room beyond slipped into the shadows and the remaining contents merged into blackness.

Sarah flicked the switch, returning the lounge to darkness, and stepped back into the passage, closing the door behind her. Nervously, she looked at the room containing the machine before continuing along the corridor.

There were several other doors dotted along the passage, none of which she decided to investigate. The final one on the right she guessed was the generator housing, as the hum she heard upon leaving the first room grew louder upon its approach.

When she reached the far end there was a sharp left which concealed a heavily fortified barrier, unseen from the opposite side.

A large circular handle, similar to those used in submarines, secured the door with what appeared to be an airtight seal. She grasped the struts running from the centre and began to turn it in an anti-clockwise direction. At first the lock held and the handle refused to move until she stepped closer and focused her strength in one area. She heard a squeak, then a groan and slowly it began to turn. For half a rotation it continued to resist until suddenly the lock loosened and the seal reluctantly released its hold on the frame.

She pushed on the door, which again had an overhanging lip to provide additional protection. It was heavy despite swinging on assisted hinges and she only opened it just enough, in her weakened state, to allow her to be able to step through.

Motion-sensitive lighting, out of place in the antiquated, elemental complex, activated to reveal a ladder travelling up a tall chute.

She entered the chamber and began to climb, but as she drew close to the halfway point, neither the light at the bottom or the light at the top reached the central section, and she had to slow down to ensure she had a firm footing in the constricting gloom before she continued on to a higher rung.

Her breathing, now sharply bouncing around in the chute, caused an echoing effect which gave the impression she was not the only one on the climb and she had to resist the urge to keep checking she was not being followed.

For several minutes she continued upwards, passing back into a lighted section before her head finally cleared the top and she was able to climb out onto a small platform, at the end of which was a door.

Sarah stepped up to the barrier.

The lever handle was deceptively simple, she realised when she pressed it down. Internal security rods withdrew into their housing in the heavy-duty metal casing surrounding the frame and the door swung outward on assisted hinges to reveal a long wide tunnel with daylight streaming in at the far end.

She stepped outside and looked around for something to hold the door open. A small rock, easily within reach, was just big enough to use as a jam. She shoved it into place, then trotted the length of the tunnel to the far end.

As she drew near to the mouth, Sarah slowed. She needed to know what was happening outside, whether she had escaped the horrific world she was prepared to die to destroy, but was terrified of what she might find. If she was still trapped, she feared she would go insane.

When Jason confessed he was a time traveller, she had thought, at first, he must be mad, then later sadly deluded, but when she materialised in the town square in Germany all her hopes of a future exploded forth with such force that it would be impossible for her to suppress them again.

She stopped, took a deep calming breath, then slowly stepped outside.

The sun was high overhead. Despite this the day lacked the brightness usually associated with midday and instead possessed a gloom more suited to dawn or dusk. The sun's rays struggled to penetrate the cloud, hanging low in the sky, still peppered with dust kicked up by the bomb.

The ground, where visible, was bare, scorched to soil level. The remainder was covered by soot smothered rubble, where once there had been houses, for as far as she could see.

She looked around, trying to gain her bearings, distracted by the sickly sweet smell which lingered in the air alongside the clinging scent of charred matter.

The entrance to the bunker was buried into the side of a hill. She stepped further out and looked up. A path to the top could be clearly seen, especially with the grass gone. She moved around and followed a trodden trail until she reached the peak, where she stopped and looked around.

She had seen the effects of the bomb on her journey from Morpeth, a few days after the attack, but had abandoned her trip about five miles from the city when it became obvious she was heading into a dead zone, but now as she looked out from one of the highest points in the region, she realised she had a clear view of ground zero.

On her left she could see the Cheviot Hills framing the horizon. At a glance all would have appeared normal as the mountains were too far away to be touched by the blast, but as her eyes drew to the near distance, she saw the decimation cause by the nuclear bomb, even as far away as ten miles from the epicentre.

At first, the damage was just superficial and the external walls and roofs of some houses could still be seen from her present location. As she moved her attention closer she saw the destruction was more than just structural when she saw some buildings, although still standing, were gutted on the edge of the fireball. Then she looked right and took in the full effects of the atomic blast.

Rubble covered the ground in all directions leading from the base of the hill. Houses were smashed, lampposts twisted, cars upturned and in amongst it all she could see the occasional piece of furniture, gnarled in the debris. The closer to the city she looked the greater the devastation: bricks became scree, scree became sand, sand became dust, until eventually all that remained was a covering of white ash where once there had been a city of office blocks, highrises, road systems and a busy river network dotted with bridges.

Initially Sarah was confused when she spotted another river flowing at diagonals to the Tyne. It was exposed when the road running over it vaporised in temperatures exceeding fifteen million degrees Celsius. She looked around, landmarks now her only guide, and soon gained her bearings due to the undulation of the surrounding hills.

The path of the river had also been altered when the downward blast had punched into the ground near the northern bank, forcing it across the riverbed and opening the Tyne out to flow across the newly formed fissure.

Sarah dropped her gaze, too shocked to cry, and made her way back down the hill. She had to find a way to reverse this. She entered the tunnel, hurried to the door and, removing the wedge, allowed it to swing shut behind her as she started down the ladder. If Briggs could use the machine to stop her correcting the timeline, then she could use the machine to stop Briggs, but she could not do it alone and knew exactly who she would have to find to help her.

Chapter Two

Nuclear Bunker, Kenton Bank Foot, Newcastle

Sarah reached the bottom of the ladder and hurried down the corridor towards the small room at the far end, only slowing as she drew near to the door. A sudden wash of anxiety gripped her as she approached the barrier. She stopped and listened for any movement from within.

If Briggs had returned and was inside the room, it would all be over. With nowhere to hide, the dangerous, powerful man would quickly overwhelm her, especially in her weakened state, and she was in no doubt she would be killed. She held her breath and listened. When a few moments passed and all remained quiet inside the room, she risked a peek and was relieved to find it was still empty.

Quickly she crossed to the table and opened the report. She scanned the contents page then turned to the relevant section which detailed how to use the machine.

She carried the booklet to the device and studied the controls. It seemed simple enough. Jason's instructions and diagrams were very clear and she could not resist a smile as she heard his 'voice' as she read the report. He had obviously written it as a guide for people who were not scientifically minded and he had done an excellent job of bringing what could have been very technical information down to the layman's level. An annotated diagram gave clear explanations of the purpose of every dial and switch, and step-by-step instructions told the user how to calculate the date, time and location of the traveller along with the amount of power required to dictate the duration of their stay. Despite this, she still felt an increasing sense of apprehension as she contemplated using the machine. The idea of being disassembled, transmitted through space and time and reassembled in another location was more than a little bit daunting.

She took a deep breath, moved to the small monitor attached to the side of the unit, touched the display and the screen, previously in 'sleep' mode, sprang to life.

A program showed the status of the machine. 'Journey 012 in progress. Traveller's return in' and a timer was counting down from fifty-five minutes.

Briggs had given himself plenty of time to carry out his deed in Germany and Sarah feared he could have done a lot more potentially irreversible damage throughout the duration of his stay.

She flicked through the report and stopped near the back. Fifty-five minutes was plenty of time to get the help she would need, especially as she knew exactly where to go.

She had no idea whether the machine would allow two separate programs to run at the same time, but there was only one way to find out.

A section, behind Jason's recommendation to destroy the machine, contained a list of global longitudes and latitudes which would allow a traveller to journey to any location on the globe.

She returned her attention to the unit. She searched through the menus, entering and leaving several screens before finally finding the system she required.

Her initial input, 55.1687°, 1.6875°, her desired destination, produced encouraging results when an icon indicated a calculation was taking place and a few seconds later a message confirmed the rotation of the Earth had been taken into consideration. Once complete, a prompt requested the length of her stay.

Her time was restricted as she would have to be back to the machine and out of the complex before Briggs returned. She set the duration to ensure she arrived at the bunker at least ten minutes before the killer came back, then initiated the program. A timer started and a countdown of twenty seconds began.

Sarah stepped up to the machine, she reached for the door and paused. A wash of panic briefly overwhelmed her and she stood a moment, her heart quickening as she battled to control her fear. She had felt the same way the first time she did this, but at least then it was Jason who had controlled the device and she was confident he knew what he was doing. She took a deep breath, stepped into the machine, closed the door behind her and waited for the sequence to commence.

She remembered the sensation was like being tickled inside, so when it came she was not at all surprised. The tingling, which travelled through her muscles all the way down to her bones, lasted only a moment before the small, brightly lit room disappeared and she found herself plunged into extremely cold darkness.

She looked around as she waited for her eyes to adjust. She could not get her bearings at first and did not recognise anything, but knew if the information she had entered into the machine was correct, she would be somewhere on the southern outskirts of Morpeth. With only forty-five minutes to do her task before she was recalled, she hoped she would not be too far away from the town centre.

As her eyes adjusted and she was able to take a better look around, she suddenly recognised her location.

A chain link fence ran off to the right of a large one-storey building opposite, and behind, another one-storey building was attached to a small two-storey house. She moved up to the fence, looked beyond and her suspicions were confirmed when she established she was standing outside of the railway station.

Sarah headed for the road and a few yards further on found the familiar British Rail sign at the entrance to the compound. She looked right and saw the street swung left down a steep hill.

She turned and began down the path as fast as she dared. The darkness, all encompassing, was made worse by the black tarmaced road and the dark stone walls holding the embankment at bay.

As she reached the bend, the decline increased and rather than having to hurry, Sarah found herself trying to slow down as gravity took ahold and her pace escalated out of control. Then suddenly she slipped.

Her arms flayed as her feet shifted, but sore, stiff muscles refused to move quickly. As she felt herself falling, she shot her head forward when she caught sight of the wall rushing up to greet her and managed to get a hand hold on the stone just in time to adjust her plummet enough to land in an ungainly heap at the base.

She scrambled to her feet and carefully moved onto the road where the blackness of the tarmac allowed her to see the patches of ice and snow more clearly.

A few minutes later she passed beneath a bridge. The sound of her breathing coming in short, sharp gasps bounced off the upward-curving bricks. Then her pace slowed when a vivid image of a young woman lying on a riverbank with a knife in her chest, buried up to the handle, reminded Sarah why she had halted her search for survivors.

She suppressed the thought and forced herself on, aware that if she encountered anyone now she would only have to deal with them for a short while as she would be recalled back to the machine in about forty minutes in any case.

At the bottom of the hill the road split into two: one heading out of Morpeth and the other leading to the town centre. The decline increased slightly as she turned right, then quickly levelled out, allowing her to pick up the pace.

The biting cold ignored her clothing, despite the layers, and she knew if she was in a bad way now, she would have been a lot worse had she been caught in this weather a week ago.

Clean clothes and a clean body were an important key to keeping warm and healthy, but in the later days, just before she met Jason, her personal care had gone downhill. She knew it was a bad sign and there was a risk there was no going back, but the depression was so deep and her situation so desperate, she could see no way out.

Then along came Jason and he fed her her first decent meal in days and her first meat-based product in a month and suddenly she started to feel better.

When he begged her to help him, the following day, she had refused and he went on to Alnwick alone. This, she felt, was her lowest point. Her physical needs had improved, but her emotional state became worse.

In his bid to get her to assist him he had forced her to face up to some harsh realities and after he left, she had to make the decision to either stay put until she died or do something to possibly change what was left of her life for the better. He had promised her he would get her life back, and if only she knew how completely literal he was being when he made that statement, she would have led the way from the building.

When she finally mustered the courage to follow him that morning, for the first time in nearly two weeks, she had washed properly, dressed warmly, then hurried after Jason to Alnwick. If he had not given her the emotional shake she needed to pull herself around, two days ago, she would have probably been dying from the cold right now.

The road swung left, then curved right and as Sarah caught her first glimpse of the town up ahead, a flutter in her stomach signalled a further twang of anxiety.

She had started to feel trapped in Morpeth, only staying out of fear, and the moment she saw the town again all the bad feelings came rushing back. Her days of cowering were long gone, though, and she knew no matter what the outcome she had to press on.

Her breathing had reached a sharp hiss by the time she crossed the bridge and turned onto the main high street on the far side of the river. She would have called out, the silence was intense so sound travelled far, but she knew she would risk alerting others to her presence.

After the war, she had spent as little time as possible outside. It was not just the radioactive dust which danced in beautiful, but deadly eddies whenever it was caught in the winds bouncing off the buildings lining the roads, but more so, the other survivors. She realised hunting for food could be hazardous when she found the body of the woman dead on the embankment. At first she had thought she was sleeping, until she drew near and saw the knife embedded in her chest. A couple of weeks later she witnessed a small group of young men with rifles using tins of food and then finally a live dog as target practice. This was enough to force Sarah into reclusion and her remaining scavenges were carried out at night.

Her watch had stopped at the point that the nuclear bomb exploded over the city of Newcastle, frying all electrical equipment within a twenty-mile radius. As time was no longer an issue, only night and day, she had never attempted to replace it with a mechanical device. A decision she now regretted. She was acutely aware the time was ticking by and she still had some distance to go, but she had no idea how long it would be before she would be returned back to the machine.

****

It was early evening before Jason finally arrived on the outskirts of Morpeth. Prior to reaching the old town, he had passed through a number of new housing estates which stretched at least a mile beyond the border. It was only his familiarity with the road system which offered assurance he was still on the right track.

Morpeth, for some reason, was a great deal larger in this timeline. The fields and forests south of the ancient town were now replaced by houses and new road systems which stretched away from the main street.

The journey took slightly longer than he anticipated and the day was drawing to an end as he arrived in the town centre.

A soft fog-like haze hung in the air. It was barely noticeable until the sun, low in the sky, neared the horizon. As the mist was illuminated, blue merged into orange, which slipped into blood red with a seamless ease that only an artist of light could achieve.

Jason became increasingly uncomfortable as the eerie rouge lengthened shadows, until finally, when the last rays of sun disappeared from sight, all the darkness pooled into one. He submitted frequently to the urge to look around when the noise of his shoes, echoing back, created the impression he was being followed. Greys blended into blacks and his eyes, of little use, picked up virtually nothing.

His urgency grew with the arrival of night. Even in familiar streets it would be difficult to find his way around in the dark. His journey through the outskirts of Morpeth had proved there were changes to the road systems and estates; therefore, any hope of finding the centre unaltered was becoming increasingly unlikely.

He broke into a trot. The library on the far side of town was his destination, but when he turned into Bridge Street and saw the building, his heart sank, for instead in its place he found the Town Hall.

Hungry, exhausted and bitterly disappointed, Jason decided he could do nothing more tonight. He would have to concentrate on finding somewhere warm and dry to sleep. He would continue with his search for the library in the morning.

The 11th century Norman church on his right, he thought, would be a good place to spend the night. It would give him time, he decided, to apologise for his tinkering and hopefully make his peace with God. As he turned to make his way towards the church, Jason stopped when he noticed a soft flickering glow coming from a first-floor window of the Town Hall.

"Just ignore her, Jason."

He turned sharply and looked at the woman.

"She's no good to you." Sarah smiled. "It's me you need to speak to."

Chapter Three

Morpeth Town Hall

Jason stepped back from the woman, alarmed. "Who are you and how do you know my name?"

"I'm Sarah." She nudged her head towards the window with the flickering light. "The same Sarah you'll find inside that room, except I'm a little bit wiser and a lot stronger – thanks to you."

"Me?" He looked at the window, then back to the woman, confused.

She stepped up, closing the gap between them. "I not only know your name, but I know exactly who you are," she said ominously.

Jason leaned back just a fraction and looked down on the small red-haired woman with the fiery green eyes. He guessed her petite frame, made smaller by the over-sized coat, was not to be underestimated; she was tough, he could tell.

"I know you're a time traveller," she stated.

His brown eyes narrowed and darkened. "How?" he asked sharply.

"I also know something went wrong," she continued, ignoring the question. "This is not your world. This is not how it should be."

His attention engaged. He knew she was right, he needed her help as he had no idea what was going on.

"You know something has gone wrong at this point, you don't know what it is, but I do."

"What happened?" Jason snapped, desperate to know.

"You accidentally killed Adolf Hitler. This stopped what would have been the Second World War, but as a result there was a nuclear war instead."

His eyes widened. "I've caused a nuclear war?" he said slowly, almost seeming to shrink.

"Yes." She twitched her shoulders. "In a sense."

He looked at the window, then turned his scrutinising, scientist's gaze back on Sarah. "So how come there are two of you?"

"That's the problem."

He snorted. "What, the fact there's been a nuclear war is not the problem?"

"No, we fixed that."

He shot out a hand. "Wait! What? *We* fixed it?"

"Yes. I'm surmising we fixed it, because there's another machine, just like the one you left in Ponteland."

He shook his head and smiled. He was having trouble getting to grips with this. "I thought time travel was bad enough, but now I'm listening to someone talking about something I haven't done yet; it's all a little bit too much to get my head around at the moment."

"The other machine is located in a bunker in a TA Centre in Kenton Bank Foot. You have two days to get there. The entrance to the bunker looks like a massive drainpipe. You'll have to be careful and quick because you'll only be a few miles from ground zero. Get into the bunker as fast as you can. I've set the timer so that I get back before Briggs returns, but there won't be much time after that."

Jason's face furrowed. "Who's Briggs?"

"A very bad man in this timeline, who I can guarantee you do not want to meet."

"How did he get my machine?"

Sarah shook her head. "I do not know. Do you know how to get to Kenton Bank Foot?"

"Yes. I grew up in the region."

"Good." She suddenly felt the tingling sensation which signalled her return. She smiled. "It's good to see you," she said softly, just before Jason disappeared.

Chapter Four

Nuclear Bunker, Kenton Bank Foot, Newcastle

Sarah shut her eyes quickly, then opened them again to a squint. A shadowy shape was standing directly ahead, but all she could see at this stage was form. No features and very little colour were offered to her overloaded retina. She stepped to the back of the machine, conditioned now to approach everything with caution. Logic dictated that the build of the person standing directly ahead was all wrong for Briggs; the height was about right, but the stockiness and breadth across the shoulders was missing, but still, it did not automatically mean it was Jason. Then as her eyes adjusted and the blurs took on a sharpened shape, she smiled with relief and reached for the door. "You found it."

"I've been here a while," Jason informed her. "A few hours. Enough time to have a really good look around. This place is incredible. There are sleeping quarters, a large kitchen, which is obviously designed to cater for a lot of people, and beyond that a massive food store with loads of tinned products. Everything I looked at was up to date, so it's not like it's an abandoned bunker." He lifted his rucksack from the ground. "I've stocked up: fish, soups and some meaty stews," he laughed, "it's at least seven kilos heavier." He looked at the machine. "So how come my time displacement unit is here?"

Sarah shook her head. "I've no idea."

"You mentioned someone called Briggs in Morpeth." Jason's face furrowed. "Who is he?"

"He's an absolute monster. He talks sweetly and smiles, but it's all an act. No warmth or kindness ever reaches his cold, grey eyes and everyone around him is terrified. Apparently he took charge of a group of soldiers who moved into Alnwick after their base was destroyed." She nodded at Jason. "We first met him when you were overheard telling me about the machine and he quizzed you about it. Later he told us we could go and that a couple of soldiers would escort us to the edge of town. As we left the main streets and drew close to the woods they confessed they had been told, by Briggs, to kill us. They said they were sick of all the killings that had taken place since he took charge and blamed him for murdering their original commanding officer. He's obviously paranoid and didn't even trust his own men, as soon after they let us go, a vicious gunfight started up on the road behind. He must have sent someone else to check on them and to confirm they carried out his orders. I don't know if somehow it's the same Briggs that was in Germany..." she stopped suddenly and thought a moment. "Hang on a minute, he looked too healthy," she said distantly.

"What?"

"He was too healthy. It can't be the Briggs from this timeline."

Jason shook his head. "I don't understand."

"The nuclear war didn't occur here last week. It happened about six weeks ago. Can you imagine what that does to the body? Everyone in this timeline has been drinking contaminated water and eating irradiated food for the past six weeks." Sarah snorted. She held out her hands, away from her body. "You've just got to look at me to see what I mean."

In the darkened streets of Morpeth, Jason had not been able to scrutinise the woman properly, but here there was no hiding anything beneath the harsh overhead lighting.

Her clothes were dirty and splattered with blood, her hair matted and dull, her left eye tinged with bruising and her lip, still swollen, was cut at the edge. There was more to it than that though, as these were things that would improve with a wash, clean clothes and a couple of days of healing, but when he looked deeper, beyond the superficial, he could see the signs of radiation poisoning. Her pale, lustreless skin, raw in patches, had broken into sores when the fibre of the tissue had started to separate and when she smiled, an angry rouge dotted with small white, puss-filled ulcers tainted her gums.

"I know Briggs was strong, but he still had that pallor about him that everyone's had since the war. That was the clue that *you* weren't from here, you looked too healthy, and it's also the clue that he isn't from here as well. That man in Germany must be from your timeline," she said firmly, "there's no other explanation for it."

"I was developing the machine for the MOD."

"Yes, well it sounds like you handed it over to the MOD and somehow this machine ended up in Briggs' hands, that is the Briggs that is obviously alive and well in your timeline." She crossed to the table and picked up the report. "This must have somehow come into his possession and he's put all the pieces together and realised you were talking about him." She handed the document to Jason.

He flicked through the pages and stopped near the end of the booklet. "This is the report I was writing alongside my research, but I haven't written the recommendation yet. So this report is from my future."

"I never left from this time machine," Sarah said, confused, "so why should I materialise in this one and not in the one I was sent from?"

Jason's mouth tightened as he thought a moment. "The other machine had no mains power and would have only had what was stored in the battery. After two days, there mustn't have been enough charge left for it to rematerialize you, so therefore you would have been recalled back to the first safe machine that was available."

Sarah turned away, her face darkening as the last moments in the basement in Ponteland ran again through her mind. The pounding at the door, the soldiers breaking in, the screaming, the gunfire and Jason's body crumbling to the ground, the top of his head blown off.

"Why didn't you just use this machine to go back to Germany and start again?"

Sarah snapped from her recall.

"Now you know this man is going to be there, you could have just gone back and stopped him."

Her face fell in exasperation. "Have you not been listening? I've just told you, he is an absolute killer." She looked down, shaking her head. "I was as naive as you until a few weeks ago." She returned her attention to the scientist, her eyes firm with fury. "You cannot underestimate how dangerous this man is. In this timeline he is a professional killer, so if the Briggs from your timeline is anything like his counterpart in this timeline then he will be every bit as dangerous and could well be even more." She looked at the machine. "Is there any way we can stop him coming back?" Suddenly her mood changed and a flash of excitement animated her features. "If we could stop him materialising he would be gone, scattered into the void of time."

"No. Even if we removed the power supply the store holds enough charge to make sure the user returns safely. I could remove the battery, but to do so I would practically have to dismantle the machine. The only way to stop him, with so little time, would be to destroy it."

Her body slumped. "And if you did that we couldn't use it to go back and undo what he, and you, have already done."

Jason nodded. "We'll have to come up with another solution." He moved around to the controls, activated the screen and his eyes widened when the display sprang to life. "According to this he's due to return in just over two minutes."

The panic which swept over Sarah's face was infectious. "We have to get out of here," she urged. She flung open the door and started down the passage.

Jason stuffed the report into his bag and followed immediately behind. He passed Sarah, weakened by radiation poisoning, a lack of food, not enough sleep and a recent major beating, with ease.

She hurried after him as fast as she could and only caught up at the door.

They had to be clear of the inner barrier before the soldier materialised. If he heard the door closing or they were caught on the ladder there was a good chance they would be killed.

Jason waited, allowing Sarah to pass and start up the chamber, before he followed behind.

As the door swung shut, a barely detectable high-pitched whine could be heard from the room at the far end of the corridor. Anyone else might have dismissed it, especially as it was so faint, but Jason knew it was the sound the machine made when it powered up.

"You have to go faster," he hissed. He looked past Sarah and saw they were only halfway to the top. "He's back in the building, we need to be out soon."

Chapter Five

Nuclear Bunker, Kenton Bank Foot, Newcastle

Briggs narrowed his eyes for a moment when he materialised in the brightness of the compact room. He waited for his pupils to adjust from night to bright before he stepped out of the machine.

He slipped his knife from its housing as he moved to the table and examined the blood-soaked blade.

When he had sliced the man's throat, it had caught for a moment on his spine, cutting into the bone. He inspected the edge for damage. There were no obvious signs, but he could not be sure and would want to sharpen it before moving on as there may not be the opportunity to do it again once he hit the road.

He pulled a handkerchief from his pocket and began to wipe the blood from the metal. Only a small portion of it came away as most of it had dried. The blade was sticky and the darkened blood had already begun to oxidise. It would need to be washed, then sharpened again with a wet stone for good measure.

A weapons store beyond the generator room contained such a tool and he needed to stock up on bullets in any case. He turned to leave the room, then stopped, his body still twisted towards the door.

Something was amiss, but he could not immediately think what. He looked at the machine, it had gone into standby mode; a small green light indicated it was still on, but apart from that the monitor was black. He touched the screen and the display lit up. Everything seemed normal. He scrolled through the list.

Journey 012, his trip, completed 16:24. He clicked on the journey below. The details opened out and confirmed this had been Jason's trip to the same location in Germany. He moved the cursor to a file positioned between the two called 'Returner'.

'Unknown Journey. Details of traveller: 117 lbs, returned 15:09.'

Briggs' face furrowed. "Who the hell are you?" he muttered. He clicked the back button to return to the list and noticed the scrollbar indicated there was more information. He moved the slider and revealed a further file, called Journey 013, previously hidden beyond the display. He opened the file and read the details.

'Traveller: 117 lbs, location: 55.1687°, 1.6875°, duration: 45 minutes, returned: 16:14.' Briggs shook his head. He did not know where that was, but knew it could not be too far away as Newcastle was located at 54° North.

Towards the back of the report there was a list of locations with their longitudes and latitudes. He looked at the table, saw the booklet was missing and his body tensed.

"Shit," he hissed. He stopped, took a deep breath and smiled. It all fell into place. "You think you're clever?" Either way it did not matter, he had a good idea of where she had been; it was in the report. He checked the time of return again and looked at his watch.

"Five minutes ago." Briggs unholstered his gun and checked the clip for bullets. It was almost full. He returned it to its housing. "You can't have gone very far in five minutes and you're going to so regret messing with me."

He strode from the room, took off along the corridor at a run, wrenched open the door and started up the ladder, two rungs at a time.

Chapter Six

Kenton Bank Foot, Newcastle

Sarah shuffled forward just enough to see beyond the drainpipe, shattered and exposed in the nuclear blast. "He's outside," she whispered, "looking around."

"Is he searching for us?"

"Yes." She ducked her head quickly back below the level of the piping and lowered herself down. "He's coming this way," she hissed, seeming to shrink and curl in on herself like a terrified child. She tugged at Jason's clothes. "Move back, deeper into the pipe."

"He can't see us," Jason insisted. "The entrance is well hidden by the bushes. *We* only found it accidentally."

She pulled harder. "We can't risk it. He'll kill us."

The pair slinked back until they merged with the darkness in the depths of the storm pipe.

There were no sounds other than the noise of their own breathing, rasping in the confines of the narrow conduit, which was barely wide enough for them both to fit.

Pressed against the woman, Jason could feel her heart pounding over his own and the gentle tremble of her muscles between each of the beats. Her breath came in stifled short gasps and when he looked down and saw her face, the darkened lines, lowered head and tightened brow revealed a terror impossible to misinterpret as anything else.

A crunching noise was heard outside the pipe and she curled in on herself further. She held her breath, her heart rate increased, thumping against Jason like a hammer.

A shadowy shape of a man, broken by the branches, passed by the bushes at the far end of the drain. He moved left, disappearing from view, then a short while later passed within sight again, some distance away, heading back in the direction of the bunker.

Sarah looked at Jason, her face dropped and pleading. "What are we going to do?"

"The moment he's gone we'll go into the bunker and fix this properly. I'll send you back with enough time so that you can stop me at the cinema. You'll be in a public place, so you'll be safe."

She shook her head. "I was in a public place last time." She looked away. "You couldn't get more public. We were surrounded by people," her voice trailed off, "and he still cut that poor man's throat."

Jason grabbed her shoulders, demanding her attention. He waited until she locked eyes with him. "He knew to go to the Havelberg Town Square because there would have been records of Hitler's activities and because I mentioned it in the report, but he's unlikely to know where the cinema is. There was no-one around when I left the picture house, the streets were empty, and I definitely wasn't followed. You'll be safe there," he added softly, "and the only person you'll meet will be an arrogant scientist called Jason."

Sarah smiled. She paused, then nodded. "OK." She looked beyond the pipe. "How will we know when it's safe to return to the bunker?"

The noise of a vehicle firing up in the distance was too much for her raw nerves and she jumped violently.

Jason raised his brows. "That could be a clue. He seems to be leaving."

For a moment the sound of the heavy diesel engine moved closer, before it swung behind them and began to fade as it travelled away.

Jason moved closer to the entrance and looked cautiously outside. He checked around for a moment before glancing over his shoulder at Sarah. "All's clear," he said. He stepped outside, pushed the bushes aside and led the way from the pipe.

They hurried to the bunker and moved inside. Pitch-blackness greeted them when the scientist opened the door.

He groped for a switch. It took some time before he finally found one. He turned it on and was horrified to find it made no difference at all and the entrance remained black.

"Hold this open," he said to Sarah. He waited for her to grab the door, then stooped and rifled through his rucksack briefly before retrieving his torch. "He must have switched off the generator." He stood. "Wait here." He activated the beam and started down the ladder.

The bunker was cold and sinister even when well lit, but now it was illuminated only by the narrow ray, it was even more unsettling.

Jason made his way slowly down the steps, the beam swinging wildly as he moved his hands lower a rung at a time, the torch gripped firmly between his thumb and index finger for fear it would fall. The noise of the metal casing clanging on the ladder echoed in the tall, narrow chamber as he stopped and looked up at Sarah. She was now nothing more than a shadowy outline, her features indistinct in the growing gloom, as the sun, already shrouded by a dense cloud, finally began to sink below the horizon.

He guessed he must be near the bottom, stopped and shone the beam to the ground.

"What's wrong?" she called.

"Just trying to see how far I have left to go," he said. He continued down the ladder and a short while later stepped off the final rung and swung the torch at the door.

The temperature had already noticeably dropped inside the bunker with the cessation of heat. It was bad enough outside, but as he had descended into the depths any kind of warmth had obviously quickly vented through the chute and it was now nearly as cold at the bottom as it had been at the top.

He turned the handle and pushed the door open. The room that housed the generator was halfway down the corridor. He was lucky he had arrived in plenty of time for Sarah's return and grew bored enough in the six-hour wait to explore the complex thoroughly.

He made his way down the passage, the light beam illuminating the floor ahead. The cold felt more acute once the inner door was closed, although he thought it may well have been his imagination. The lights added some warmth, no matter how small, to the bare concrete corridor and the psychological effect of the gentle hum of the motor could also not be ruled out.

He reached the room that housed the unit and stepped inside.

The generator was protected from the electromagnetic pulse, produced when the atomic bomb detonated over the city of Newcastle-upon-Tyne, by the nuclear bunker. As a result, it had to be vented into the outside world by an exhaust running into the wall. The fuel-powered device was otherwise started with a key.

Jason swept the beam over the casing with increasing anxiety when all he could find was an empty lock. "Come on, come on. Where are you?" he squawked. He moved around the unit and studied it from all angles, hoping to find the key placed or hanging somewhere on the device. With no success, he started to search the floor. A few minutes after, when he had all but lifted the generator to hunt beneath, he had to admit that the key was gone and was no doubt with Briggs.

He returned to the corridor and hurried down the passage to the room which contained the time machine. Inside, he moved to the monitor and touched it to activate the display. The battery would be fully charged and there should be enough power to return Sarah so she could stop him as he came out of the cinema.

The system started up and four lines of code appeared in the top left of the screen. Something was wrong. The menus were missing. Even the prompt to enter further commands was unavailable, so he would not be able to run the programs manually. He switched off the machine then turned it back on to force it to reboot.

The system started, passed the initialisation point, the display changed and returned to the screen with the four lines of code.

He switched off the unit to save power, moved around to the far side and saw a door leading into the workings of the device standing open.

He snorted. Briggs had made no attempt to hide his tampering. Why should he? He had all the power. The only advantage they had at this stage was that he was unaware of the scientist's involvement. 'For what it's worth,' Jason thought cynically.

He stepped in front of the panel and sat back on his heels, thoroughly regretting being so detailed with the information he gave with the unit.

The schematics were inside the report passed over to the MOD, so Briggs would have been able to find his way around the system easily. He would not have needed a detailed knowledge of the workings of the machine to have been able to sabotage it.

He lit up the inside of the device. At first there was no sign of any tampering, then suddenly he spotted a small circuit board missing towards the back of the system. It was a simple pop in, pop out chip which could easily be removed and returned by Briggs whenever he needed to disable or use the machine again. It was as good as a key or a lock any day.

Jason popped a neighbouring chip out of its seating and slipped it into his pocket. "Not so smart now, are you? I need you and you need me," he muttered.

He stood, desperation and depression taking hold, and turned to leave the room. He would have to return to Sarah and tell her the bad news, then they would have to try to come up with another plan which did not involve a potentially suicidal confrontation with Briggs. He stopped and looked back towards the table.

A sheet of paper sat where previously there had been the report. He moved closer to see what was written on it. It was folded in half with 'FAO: Sarah' scrawled in large letters across the front.

A lump instantly formed in Jason's throat and he felt the need to swallow to attempt to dislodge it. He opened up the sheet and read the quickly written note inside.

"You'll never save her as I already have a head start, so don't even try. If I kill the other Sarah, what do you think will happen to you? You should have stayed out of my business, bitch!"

Jason hurried from the room and sprinted the length of the passage.

"I was getting worried," Sarah called when she heard the door open and saw the torch beam light up the bottom steps. "What's wrong," she gasped when she saw Jason's fear, her voice echoing loudly in the chamber.

He never spoke, he simply kept climbing, the need to get out of the bunker fast overriding every other thought.

"He's booby trapped the place, hasn't he?" she shrieked as the scientist drew closer, his panic now infectious.

Jason looked up, close enough to the top to feel he was nearly out. "No, it's worse than that. We have to hurry, he's going to do something really terrible."

Chapter Seven

Nuclear Bunker, Kenton Bank Foot, Newcastle-upon-Tyne

Jason left the ladder almost at a sprint.

"He's going to do what?" Sarah squawked.

"He's going to try to kill you in Morpeth." He flung open the outside door and led the way from the complex with Sarah immediately behind. "We have to try to find some transportation."

She struggled to keep up and was a few paces behind by the time they emerged outside. "Nothing works," she panted, "there's been a nuclear war, remember."

Jason stopped, thought a moment. "Of course. The electromagnetic pulse." He pointed, "But Briggs had a car. He must have protected a vehicle from the effects of the bomb." He looked around. "I remember this place. There was a Territorial Army Centre here. It must have been an army vehicle he used. Come on. There might be more nearby."

He turned right from the pipe and followed the path of the small hill which acted as a buffer to protect the structure from the shockwave of the bomb.

The side of the mound, which faced the city, was scorched to soil level when the firestorm desiccated and then ignited the grass in an instant.

"We're wasting time," Sarah gasped, the distance between them drawing greater as she struggled to exert herself above a walk. "We'll never catch him up. It's hopeless." She stopped and burst into tears.

Jason halted and faced her. "It's not hopeless. He might have a head start on us, but he doesn't necessarily know where you are."

She inhaled sharply, her breath coming in juddering gulps. Slowly, she calmed. "You're right." She pointed to Jason's backpack. "I skimmed through your report and I remember you mentioned you met me in Morpeth, but you never said where."

"Excellent. There you go." He smiled. "We could still reach you before he does. Come on; there'll be no giving up. I can't imagine a man like Briggs not having a backup plan for getting out of here." He nudged his head upward. "Help me find where he hid that vehicle and let's see if there's another one."

The pair continued around the hill and at the far side were delighted to find a large door buried in the soil. Inside the bigger structure was a smaller door which allowed personnel to enter without the need to open the main hangar.

Jason approached the opening and tried the handle. "It's locked." He was not surprised. He glanced around for something to use as a lever.

The debris field caused by the nuclear explosion was vast. Houses lay in ruins in the immediate vicinity and for up to two miles north away from the site, but still there was nothing suitable instantly at hand.

"Stay here," he instructed.

Sarah stepped up to the door as she watched Jason moving away. Huddled in a corner, she found some protection from the cold. A slight breeze, which gathered itself into gusts from time to time and dropped the single figure temperatures to nearly zero, could not quite make it into the corner and only managed to tug at her clothing around the cuffs and fringes.

Jason made his way in the direction of the road, more out of habit than anything else. Even at a distance he could see the unmistakable markers of an ordered track, exposed occasionally from beneath bricks, shattered furniture, wood and slates.

He could not tell whether it was glass or frost that was sparkling in the failing light; either way, it crunched under foot and seemed to cover everything on his route to the tarmaced trail.

Once on level ground Jason quickly found his way blocked by destroyed homes. Mounds of bricks, snapped wood and twisted piping were piled almost to the height of the original structures. He switched on his torch, the murk becoming an issue, and searched through the rubble for something to use as a lever.

There was plenty of plastic piping and wood that was too thick to use as a wedge, but he was frustrated to find it surprisingly difficult to locate something long enough and strong enough for the required job. His growing urgency did not help. Drifting into a state of panic, he was sweeping the torch beam rather than carefully searching and when he skidded on a plank of wood, slippy with frost, and nearly fell onto a pane of glass broken into jagged points, he knew he had to slow his exploration and calm down before they found themselves trapped in this hellish world for ever simply because he had a stupid accident. He focused his mind and was soon delighted when a short time later the torch beam fell on a solid metal bar the width of his thumb.

He grabbed the object and tried to lift it, but it was weighed down by something hidden beneath a sheet of corrugated metal. Jason released the bar and lifted one end of the dislodged plate and flipped it over to see what was holding the rod in place. He returned his attention to the shaft and instantly recoiled in horror when he saw it buried in the stomach of a woman.

She wore a white cardigan over a pastel blue cotton dress, dotted with daisies. Her clothes were splattered with mud and covered in a fine coating of black ash and were soaked to her skin, where rainwater had pooled beneath the body. Her face, drawn tight against her skull, was shrivelled, dark grey and was sunken at the cheeks and eyes. She did not appear to have been burned, despite the bricks near the body being blackened along one side, and must have been protected by the house when the bomb exploded. Instead, she seemed to have been crushed when the building was destroyed; a gaping hole in her scalp, which revealed the skull beneath, provided possible proof of this hypothesis.

Jason returned the corrugated metal to cover the body and continued his search for another lever.

He moved on deeper into the rubble, picking his way over mounds of crumbled bricks and shattered furnishings. Skimming the wreckage, he looked, but not too deeply, now fearful of what he might find.

On his left, a leg protruding from beneath a crushed chair alerted him to look sharply right. Further on a mass of matted hair, grey skin stained with blood from the eyes, mouth and nose, prompted another quick change of direction.

This time, though, the new route proved to be a good one as he had a lucky find when he caught his foot on something as he returned to the grassy bank. Looking down he saw it was another, slightly heavier and thicker bar, more suited to the task. He picked it up and hurried back to Sarah.

“It’s slightly longer than I would have liked, but we can’t afford to be choosy. You’d think...” his voice became strained as he jammed one end of the split pole into the small gap in the door near the lock, “that in the rubble left over from the destruction of at least a hundred houses, there would be quite a few substantial objects you could break into a...” he paused to add a bit more weight against the rod, briefly unable to speak as he forced his body against it, “high-security facility with.”

A loud groan confirmed Jason was making progress. Briefly, the metal buckled near the lock and just as he thought the rod might be the one to give first, the frame snapped and the door popped open.

He flung the bar off to one side. It made a noise like someone had just hit it with a rubber hammer before rolling a short distance away and coming to a silent halt up against a pile of soft mud.

Jason opened the door to reveal blackness concealed the contents of the room beyond. He switched on the torch and swept the beam ahead. “Wow! What a find.” He stepped inside with Sarah immediately behind.

“Do you think it’ll start?” Sarah stopped beside one of the five army jeeps dotted about the warehouse.

“I would imagine this building would have additional shielding for this very reason.”

“We’ll not exactly be able to sneak into Morpeth in a jeep, remember there are no other noises: no aeroplanes, no cars, not even any people,” she shrugged, “well not many anyway. There’ll be nothing to disguise the sound of an engine.”

A line of keys hung on hooks above a long wooden bench littered with engine parts. Jason crossed to examine them. They were all colour coded, but without a corresponding chart it would be down to trial and error. He followed the line, searching for one that looked like it might be suitable for a vehicle. Some of the keys could be instantly disregarded as they were obviously not designed for cars, but when he came to a cluster that looked like they were used to start up an engine, he looked over his shoulder at Sarah. "Can you see some colour coding on any of the jeeps?" He held his hand high to light up the nearest car and waited whilst she searched the bodywork for any markings.

She circumnavigated the vehicle, then shook her head. "There's nothing here."

"Try looking inside."

She leaned forward and peered through the driver's window, paused a moment, then stood. "There is a small blue mark circling the ignition."

Jason returned to the hooks and found a key with a glossy blue splodge of what looked like nail varnish on the handle. He removed it from the hanger and moved to the car beside Sarah. "We don't have to be discreet," he told her, "we just have to be quick. As long as he doesn't find you first, then we should be in and out before he can stop us." He slipped the key into the lock then looked at her with a satisfied smile when he turned it and was rewarded with a distinct click.

Chapter Eight

Morpeth

Briggs took the Telford Bridge, which crossed the River Wansbeck on the outskirts of Morpeth Town Centre, at speed. The gentle hump would cause a more cautious driver to slow slightly to keep the vehicle stable, but not the aggressive warrior who was completely unfazed when for a moment all four wheels were airborne before they re-engaged with the road in time for him to make the turn at the roundabout on the far side. He swung left, his main beam lighting up the front of the terraced houses which had been converted into businesses in the early part of the twentieth century, and entered the main high street. He drew to a halt in the middle of the road, switched off his lights and scanned the windows for signs of life.

Jason had not stated in his report where he had found Sarah, but he had mentioned a window glowing from the light of a nearby fire had been his first connection with the woman.

The ancient town had houses which dated back to the 16th century, all of which would have been heated solely by open fireplaces. He had no doubt there would be a number of properties suitable for occupation in a post-apocalyptic world and if anything they may well be at a premium.

Briggs stepped out of the vehicle and waited for his eyes to adjust to the blackness of the night before looking in both directions as far as he could see.

The fronts of the houses remained engulfed in darkness. The only fluctuations offered to his eyes were the different tones and shades of the cold bricks, stone and windows, all of which remained black within their frames.

He popped open the back and slipped a night vision torch from his belt. The soft red glow emitted by the device was just enough to illuminate the interior for Briggs to find what he was looking for. He retrieved the device, closed the boot and activated the hand-held thermal camera.

Slowly, he moved the front of the unit up the street. The screen remained dark and cold, with no heat sources revealed until halfway up the road an alley appeared in the range of the scope and the display changed colour.

A living entity glowed hotly in the centre of the camera. Briggs lowered the unit, but his eyes picked up nothing other than the all-encompassing night. The source was quite small and, if human, would likely be a child, but still there was a chance it could be an adult huddled up on the ground. He moved to investigate it further and got no closer than seven yards, enough for the entity to begin to take form, before suddenly a fox rose from a crouched position and hurried across the road, carrying a small animal that looked like the remains of a rabbit.

He watched it move up the street then turn onto a road that travelled down towards the river.

The Wansbeck, a wide deep river which ran south of the main high street, was well populated by ducks and swans in better times and Briggs now wondered how many still remained. Six weeks after the nuclear war, he guessed that most food sources would have probably run out and the people who had stayed in the region would now be desperate enough to have to start hunting for themselves. The ducks and swans, who were used to being fed by hand, would be an easy target and any that were still alive now would be a lot more cautious than they would have possibly been two months ago.

He continued with his sweep. A few minutes later he had completed a scan of the whole street and the camera had remained cold.

He returned to the car, removed a map, identified Bridge Street and put a cross on the page. He climbed back into the vehicle, started the engine and drove to the top of the road where he stopped and repeated the process again.

A short while later he returned to the car, when the camera stayed dark, and continued up on to Newgate Street. As he drove up the road his lights briefly illuminated a number of brown and red stains on the tarmac. As he passed the spot a cluster of empty tins, which had rolled into the gutter, caught up in the wake of his wheels, clattered and span until they ran out of momentum and settled once again further down the hill.

Two hundred yards on he turned right at a junction and joined a road which ran around the northern edge of the town. There he stopped, scanned the shops, small terraced houses and upstairs flats, before returning to the car and driving on again. A swing in the road had taken the buildings beyond the range of the camera. He rounded the bend and halted to check the row of dwellings which had been beyond the reach of the scope. He stepped out of the vehicle and looked ahead.

A mismatch of old and new lodgings stood side by side when spaces in the older part of the town were utilised. Dotted in amongst the Georgian and Victorian houses, terraces and official premises was the occasional new build which now occupied grassy areas big enough to fit the purpose.

Briggs turned to reach for the camera, then stopped. At first he thought he may have imagined it, but when he looked again he realised he was correct and there was a faint glow coming from the grand 18th century building fifty yards ahead on the right. He reached for the heat detector and pointed the scope at the upstairs window, then smiled when a warm, flickering flush appeared in the centre of the screen.

He returned to the back of the vehicle, popped open the boot and put the camera back into its casing. He unclipped the small LED night vision light and attached it to a strap at the back of the enclosure, then released a large box secured with Velcro tape and opened the lid.

The container spread out into three parts to reveal an array of weapons. First from the box was a belt, which he fastened around his waist. Next was a semi-automatic, which he loaded with a clip and slotted into its housing near the buckle. Two knives followed: the first was a small neck dagger, which was placed into a holster inside his jacket, and the second was a fixed combat blade with a serrated edge along one side, which was slotted into a sheath tied against his leg. Finally, Briggs retrieved a small handgun. He checked the chamber for bullets before holstering it into his coat on the opposite side to the knife. He grabbed a handful of extra clips, popped them into a small bag settled on the belt at the base of his spine, switched off the light and closed the boot. He locked the car, then strode towards the building.

As he drew closer, the glow from the window became more distinct. A soft orange flicker, from a nearby, but out-of-view source, licked up the glass and across the frame. Its effect was pleasing and psychologically it seemed to lift the bitter cold even from the street.

He looked for a way in. The large double doors appeared to be firmly closed, but when he stepped up and tried the handle, he was delighted to find they were actually unlocked.

He pushed against the wood then stopped when a slight groan was amplified by the inner chamber. He continued more slowly, controlling the swing until the door was wide enough to step through before he entered the building, then turned and closed the barrier behind him.

A large open foyer covered in stone tiles was lit gently by the light from a half moon, revealed when the clouds began to clear.

A reception desk was on the left and across the hall two staircases led to the upper floors.

He quickly scanned the area, confirming he was alone, before moving away from the safety of the door and heading up to the next level.

A long passage on the first floor landing led off to the right.

The upper floor was carpeted, unlike the foyer, so he was unconcerned about the risk of being heard. Still, he prowled rather than walked the corridor, carefully placing his feet until he drew close to a door, where he slowed further when a faint glow bleeding beneath the base confirmed this was the room he had seen from the street.

He stopped outside and was just about to ready his gun when, "Who the fuck are you?" came from behind.

Briggs spun around to find a man, carrying a torch, halfway down the passage. Quickly he assessed the situation.

He appeared to be returning from the washroom as he carried a bar of soap and had a towel draped over his left arm. Although he was fully dressed, Briggs could not see a weapon. Despite this he knew he would have to act fast, as there was a chance the man was not alone and might call out to alert his friends that he was being attacked.

He seemed shocked to see Briggs and despite his outward bravado, had stopped for a moment, keeping his distance away from the soldier. He recovered quickly, though, and moved swiftly down the corridor to confront the renegade face to face. "I'm speaking to you," he said aggressively. "Who the fuck are you?"

His confidence had grown and Briggs guessed there was a chance this indicated there were others nearby, more than likely inside the room. He had to silence the man quickly before he was discovered.

Briggs stepped up, closing the gap between them to just a few yards.

"Stay where you are," the man ordered. He dropped his toiletries and reached for his belt.

For a moment Briggs saw the glint of a gun, previously concealed by the towel, caught in the light from the torch.

Fumbling briefly, his motor functions unaccustomed to automatically finding the weapon, the man cast his eyes down.

This was the move Briggs was waiting for.

The last of the man's life was composed of sounds rather than sight. The soft hiss of the blade being extracted from the sheath, the gentle whoosh as it flew through the air and the thud as it impacted his chest, stopping his heart immediately. He crumbled to the ground, hitting his head off the wall as he went down.

Briggs stepped up to the body, placed a foot onto the young man's chest, gave the knife a twist to release the vacuum and extracted it from the body. He picked up the towel and wiped the blade clean.

"Hey, Rob!" a distant voice called. "You all right?"

Briggs returned the knife to its sheath, unholstered his semi-automatic, moved to the door and stepped into the room.

Chapter Nine

Telford Bridge, Morpeth

Jason drove over the Telford Bridge on his way into Morpeth, stopped at the roundabout and looked right.

"What are you doing," Sarah snapped, irate. "There's nothing coming." She raised her hands, exasperated. "There's never anything coming, EM pulse, remember."

He shook his head. "I can't get used to it." He slipped the jeep into gear and stalled the engine. "Damn." Quickly he went to start the car again and was just about to turn the key when the sound of gunfire echoed through the previously silent streets.

The pair looked at each other, panicked.

"Hurry and don't stop at every junction," Sarah urged, her words catching in her throat. "Apart from us there is nothing else on the roads except for the military."

He revved up the engine, then floored the accelerator. The wheels for a moment were unable to get a grip and span, stripping rubber onto the road, before finally they gained enough traction for the vehicle to leap forward.

"The military?" Jason called.

The jeep had a very basic design and was equipped with the barest of soundproofing. As a result the compartment was quite noisy.

Sarah filled in the gaps. "When we travelled back to Ponteland a lorry passed us on the road. Because it was so quiet we could hear it coming from miles away. We hid in a ditch until it passed by, but as it drew near we could see into the carriage. The compartment light was on and there were three men inside. They were all wearing white overalls and one of them was obviously injured. He lay with his head against the side window and his chest was soaked in blood. They were driving an army lorry and were towing a trailer behind with some seriously heavy artillery inside: rockets, bazookas, attack rifles, stuff like that."

Sarah went silent. She felt herself lurch towards the gear stick and grabbed the armrest on the door to steady herself as the car swung sharply left around a tight bend in the road. She looked across at Jason. "You didn't seem too surprised and appeared to know what was going on. When I tried to quiz you on it you were reluctant to give me any more details, except to tell me that you thought Briggs would be too busy dealing with disgruntled, heavily armed townspeople to be bothering us any more."

Jason screwed up his face and shook his head slightly. "It's so weird. You keep saying stuff I know nothing about; stuff I didn't do, like it was me, when it wasn't me. I feel like I should know; it's like I have amnesia or something."

They rounded another bend and he drew the jeep to a halt.

"Why are you stopping?" She waved a hand at the window. "The Town Hall is in the next street along."

Jason unbuckled his seatbelt and started from the car. "Parking the jeep at the door would be foolish. It would be obvious we've arrived and wouldn't just give our location away, but that of your counterpart as well. If he still can't find her, he may just turn his attention to trying to kill us instead. We need to be discreet. We travel on foot from here."

She stepped from the vehicle, quietly closed the passenger door and followed Jason on to the road. They travelled at a trot through the darkened, silent streets.

"It's amazing the difference that short sleep has made," Sarah said as she broke into a run. "What was it..? Twenty minutes, yet already I've got a lot more energy."

"You went straight into a deep sleep," Jason informed her, "that'll be why. My only worry was, if you woke up feeling sick," he glanced around at her, "but you seem OK."

"Yes, I'm fine." She smiled. "I could have done with another ten hours, of course, but you get what you can."

They followed the line of houses and small perfectly manicured gardens, stunted in their emergence from their annual hibernation by the onset of a nuclear winter, which halted the return of spring.

By the time they reached the end of the road, the exertion was catching up with Sarah. “Wait!” she panted. She stopped alongside a narrow lane leading to a string of garages.

Jason halted a few paces ahead, his breathing just starting to quicken.

“We don’t have to join the main street.” She pointed. “We can cut through this alley and it’ll take us out onto the top end of the road, which runs directly in front of the Town Hall.” She led the way.

Refuse was strewn along the narrow lane, where an occasional bin, left out for a collection that never happened, had toppled, spilling its contents onto the ground. A scattering of paper, tins and bottles made the journey through the dark passage extremely hazardous. The noise of waste crunching under foot was interlaced by the clatter of rolling glass and tinkle of metal, when the pair accidentally kicked the debris littering the lane.

“I quickly learned how to get around whilst avoiding the main routes in the early days after the war. I was desperate at first to find other survivors, but when I found the body of a murdered woman down by the river, I became very quiet and did everything I could to avoid being seen from that point on.”

Jason looked at her, shocked. “Were there many people in the area? Do you think there was only one killer or do you think there were a few involved?”

“I don’t know. In the weeks that followed I witnessed a frightening level of brutality. I saw men being beaten and killed for not burying the dead fast enough and a dog being used as target practice by some drunken youths. And then there was Briggs and his second-in-command, Andrews, who took the brutality and horrors up to another level altogether.” She shook her head. “You don’t recover from that.”

“I’ll bet,” Jason said quietly. He waved a hand as they neared the end of the alley. “Slow down,” he instructed.

They slowed to a walk, then stopped just short of joining the road and peered out.

“Which way is the Town Hall?”

Sarah leaned forward and pointed left.

The scientist followed the direction of her finger up the straight road. He paused, then said, “I can’t really see much, but there don’t appear to be any cars parked up the street.” He stepped into the open. “Come on, let’s move a bit closer.”

Jason ran ahead, with Sarah trailing slightly behind. He could see the building’s black outline against the stars. He ran swiftly on his toes to avoid making a noise, until he drew close enough to get a clear view of the road at the front, then waited for Sarah to catch up. “There’s nothing outside.”

“He could have done what we’ve done and parked in a nearby street,” she panted.

“True. We have to go inside; all we can do is be careful. We’ll have to presume he’s there, but hope that he’s not.”

They hurried up the steps leading into the building and quietly slipped in through the front door.

They scanned the foyer to check it was empty, whilst Jason retrieved his gun, then headed for the stairs when they were satisfied there was not an ambush taking place.

“If anything happens let me deal with it,” he whispered.

"You're a pretty good shot with that gun," she confirmed, "but you're not so good with your fists."

Jason glanced at her, bemused. "Fists?"

"I got captured in the library in Alnwick, by Briggs' men. I was tied up, beaten and interrogated in the basement. Then you rescued me."

The corners of Jason's mouth twitched as a rush of pride caught him off guard. He had never considered himself a coward, but would never describe himself as being brave, but here he was being told how, despite serious danger, he had saved Sarah from pain, torture and possible death.

"We got to the top of the stairs, had just left the basement and we were attacked," she continued.

Then the bubble burst.

"You tried to punch your way out of it, but despite swinging your fists three times you only ever hit air. Andrews easily dodged you, it was almost like he was playing, before he got bored and knocked you out." She looked at Jason deliberately. "Do not try to take this man on," she said firmly. "He is a professional killer, we will run, hide, do anything, but please don't think you can take him on in a fight."

Jason nodded slowly. "OK."

They stopped just short of the landing and Jason leaned forward to check it was clear. He moved back, mouthed, 'it's empty,' then stepped off the stairs.

Sarah grabbed his arm. She pointed left when he looked around, then moved behind as the scientist led the way from the hall and entered a passage running off the landing.

A small amount of light had illuminated the upper level from the narrow windows running along the top of the walls, but as they entered the corridor they were plunged into almost complete darkness. Jason moved on a few more paces then stopped and rummaged through his bag before finally emerging with his torch.

"You can't use that," Sarah hissed, "we'll be seen."

"I'm only going to switch it on briefly to see if there's anyone hiding at the end of the passage," Jason whispered. "We'd be trapped and an easy target if we were to go down there and discover someone was waiting. Get ready to run," he warned. He held his finger poised over the torch switch, then touched on and off in close succession. The wall at the far end lit up dimly, for just a moment, but enough to see that the remainder of the corridor was empty.

They passed a number of rooms on both sides of the hall and she felt Jason twitch in anticipation every time they closed in on another door. Each time she urged him on with a gentle push on his back until they drew near to the end of the passage. "It's the last door on the right," she whispered close to his ear, her breath gently tickling the nape of his neck.

He stopped outside of the indicated room and grabbed the door handle. He looked back. "It's freezing."

Sarah reached around and touched the wood. She looked up. "I always kept the fire going to keep the room warm. This door feels stony cold. I suspect there's been no heat in that room for some time and I'm not talking hours, more like days."

"Get behind me," Jason instructed. He waited until Sarah moved before he turned the handle and stepped into the room. He wanted to go first, not just because of the danger, but more from fear of what they might find.

His eyes had adjusted to the darkness of the corridor so the office seemed bright in comparison.

The moon had emerged from behind its cloudy shroud to illuminate the curtainless room to the level of dusk.

Shadowy images from chairs and tables were cast like monstrous fingers across the floor towards the door as if there was an attempt to escape the deathly cold within.

"The fire's out." He stepped away from the frame, moving a little further in. "Wait here." He took a good look around, confirmed there was no-one hiding, or otherwise, then beckoned Sarah in behind.

She crossed to the fire, picked up the poker and shoved it amongst the ashes. "I can't say how long it's been out, but it doesn't look like it's been used today." She returned the rod to its stand beside the hearth and turned to face the scientist. "A group of lads that were looking for anything to use as target practice after they raided the gun shop at the top of the high street made me nervous when I heard them firing their guns off near the Town Hall. The food was starting to run low and I think they were hunting in the grounds out back. A family of deer were getting brave now that the streets had gone quiet and I'd seen them one morning wandering through the supermarket car park, which was near the woods. If *I'd* seen them, there's a good chance the guys with the guns had seen them as well."

"How many were there in the group?"

"I never saw more than five together, but there might have been more. Either way, when I realised they were hunting nearby it made me nervous so I decided I'd be better off moving to the other side of town. There was a mock castle-style Tudor mansion, with a heavily fortified front door which appeared to still be empty. The chimneys looked like they were in use, some of these old houses had their fires boarded up because they were just a source of draughts, so I would have been able to warm the rooms." She looked around. "And, unlike this place, which was designed as a public building from the start, this was a family home so therefore there would have been bathrooms. Although I wouldn't have had hot running water, I could at least have a proper bath, heated with a boiled kettle, and would be able to sleep in a bed again instead of trying to get comfortable on these couches every night." She dropped her eyes, her mouth quivering. "My health was going into decline; I hoped if I could at least get a decent sleep it might help some." She looked up and gave a slight smile. "Then you came along," and just as quickly, it was gone, "but this other Sarah never met you and she would still be fighting to survive alone."

Jason touched her arm. "Terrified, starving and radiation poisoning, I'm not surprised you were going into decline. Do you think that gunfire we heard as we came into town could have just been those lads hunting?"

She raised her brows. "It's a possibility." She brightened slightly.

"Come on." Jason nudged his head towards the door. "Take me to this other place and we'll make sure your counterpart is safe."

Sarah led the way from the room and a short while later the pair emerged outside.

A frosty sheen glistened like a sprinkling of silver dust in the moonlight on the tarmaced road beyond the building.

"Is it very far from here?" Jason asked.

"About half a mile."

"Would it be quicker to get the jeep?"

"Yes. It's pretty much a straight route, so we could get there really fast."

They started back towards the vehicle, turned into the alley and hurried along the cobbled lane towards the street where they had left the car.

As they neared the halfway mark and caught their first clear view of the road ahead, Jason thrust a hand out in front of Sarah. "Wait," he urged.

She stopped. "What's wrong," she gasped.

He bundled her towards the narrow paths running alongside the garages lining the alley, the need to hide suddenly becoming an irresistible drive. There he stood listening, his eyes distant as he focused on a remote sound. "I can hear an engine."

Sarah tilted her head slightly back, trying to control her breathing, which was drowning out all other noises. She paused, listening, before, "Yes, I can hear it as well. It seems to be moving away." She looked at Jason. "Do you think that's Briggs?"

"I'm sure of it," he said firmly. "We never saw another vehicle throughout our entire journey and you said yourself there is nobody else on the roads except for the military." He waited a moment for the sound of the engine to fade, before, "Come on," he said, leading the way.

A short while later they trotted out of the alley and came to an abrupt halt when they caught sight of the car up ahead.

For a moment they stood in silence, both too shocked to move or speak, unable to comprehend what they were seeing and yet, at the same time, powerless to tear their eyes away.

"Stay here," Jason said huskily. He felt sick.

Sarah waited for him to move away. He only travelled a few paces before, unable to resist, she continued following behind.

He crossed the road and approached the jeep, which remained exactly where they had left it.

The damage to the vehicle was obvious even from across the street, but it was not the slashed tyres and smashed windscreen that focused Jason's attention, it was the body sprawled across the bonnet.

Forcing himself on, he approached the jeep, walking robotically. In a shock-filled haze he looked on as if through someone else's eyes. He wanted to run as far away as he could, never stopping until his lungs ached and the image that lay before him was burned from his mind.

He looked at the army boots, laced up to the calf, a little closer and he focused on the pants. They were slightly padded for extra warmth and were tucked into the boots to keep out the drafts.

The legs hung across the grill from the knees as though they had been sitting on the bonnet and had just decided to lie down.

Closer again and he could see the warm jumper had ridden up, exposing the edge of a vest and a good portion of abdomen. The stomach almost concave and protruding hips were coloured with bruising. Jason stopped and moved his eyes up. The arms were spread and attached to the frames on either side of the windscreen with cable ties. His eyes came down and moved central.

The throat had been cut and it seemed on the bonnet of the car that blood, black in the moonlight, had spilled over the metal, poured from the hood and pooled on the road beneath the vehicle.

He looked at the face. Tape had been placed over the mouth to stop them screaming out. The green eyes were wide and lifeless and the auburn hair soaked with blood. "Sarah," he gasped.

"I told you he was ruthless."

Jason jumped; he did not think she was right behind him. He dragged his eyes away from the scene and turned to the living double. He took her by the arm and moved away from the car. "He obviously thinks by killing you here he will have destroyed your entire existence. What he doesn't realise is that you are now a woven part of the German timeline and the only way to stop that is to kill you there."

"So you think he'll now presume I'm dead."

"Yes, and he's completely unaware of my presence," Jason added. "He'll be happily getting on with his own plans, thinking nothing can stop him now. I would suggest our next move would be to go to Ponteland and see if we can get some power to use the machine there and if not, then we can get the same part that Briggs took from the other machine in the bunker, start that one up and go back and sort out this mess once and for all. I would suggest as we are again on foot we'd better get a move on."

Chapter Ten

En-route to Alnwick

Briggs smiled as he pulled off the Morpeth slip road and joined the motorway at speed. 'That's one little irritant gone,' he thought. 'Now for the next.'

He turned onto the A1, straightened out the vehicle, then floored the accelerator and climbed to speeds which far exceeded the legal limit in peace time. The road was straight and wide and with no other traffic to worry about, Briggs could travel at velocities he would otherwise consider dangerous under the circumstances.

He was aware that medical care would not have exactly been thrust back to the dark ages, but would still be limited. Hospitals could be powered by generators for as long as there was fuel and there would be antibiotics, until they ran out. Eventually, though, equipment would break, specialists would die and, with surviving a priority over education, the medical system would slip back to something that was akin to two hundred years ago.

The motorway normally glowed brightly with tall lamps illuminating the carriages to minimise the risk of accidents, but with the power out, the way ahead was black and the jeep's main beam, which had been set to maximum, was the only source of artificial light in the immediate vicinity.

Briggs glanced at his watch, lit in the gentle backlight of the dash. It was approaching midnight. It was ten miles to Alnwick and he wanted to arrive soon. He had a vague plan, but wanted to get there when everyone, apart from the occasional sentry, was asleep. He needed time to hunt down his target and get him out of the way before dawn, so he could take up his position in the team.

His body began to settle, coming down from the rush he felt when he had killed the woman. It was not as if she had been a threat, it was just simply she was in his way. It was important he succeeded and her life was considered nothing compared to his.

He reached for the radio and, not thinking, switched it on. The gentle hiss of background radiation filled the compartment instead of music. Briggs twiddled the dial, searching for a reception. He went through the whole bandwidth before he finally gave up and switched it back off.

He furrowed his brow and thought about the wisdom of what he was doing. Everything had now changed. Things he had taken for granted would not necessarily be available to him ever again. He had thought he had thought it through, but now that here he was unable to get something as simple and global as a radio reception, he found himself surprised. He had accepted his world would change, but had thought more in terms of food and medicine.

Surprise was the closest thing to shock Briggs ever got. Shock was an emotion he was not capable of, his mother would say; it was usually him doing the shocking.

He had not spoken to his mother for fifteen years before her death. They had stopped speaking around about the time that his father died. His father had died suddenly from head injuries following a car accident and his mother would not believe him when he said he was not able to attend the funeral due to work.

In the run up to his mother's death his sister had begged him, when she only had hours left to live, to come to the hospital to make his peace, but it had meant cancelling a lunch appointment which had been organised for weeks, so he never went. Not that he would have gone in any case. 'Cold fish' is what his mother had called him. They never had much of a relationship. She looked after him out of duty rather than motherly love, she confessed in later years, so he was happy to stay away and did not think she would have appreciated him visiting her in any case. She loved Angie; his sister was always the favourite.

Angie had insisted on keeping in touch, no matter how hard he tried to shake her off. She was a beautiful, kind and loving creature, or so he was told. She asked questions he could not answer and pried into his life in a way that was annoying. He was happiest focusing on his career rather than family. Relationships made him uncomfortable. That was an emotion he had to deal with, so it was easier to simply stay away. Angie was the only one left now and even she seemed to be finally getting the message.

The time displacement unit at Kenton was his emergency plan. If he did need medical treatment he could always go back to before the nuclear war and visit a hospital then. Using the machine, he could go anywhere in the world for his treatment and would not just be restricted to the United Kingdom. If his illness was more sinister and he required more specialised, modern care, such as if the radiation caught up with him despite his use of iodine tablets, he could always return to Germany and kill Jason to correct the timeline himself, but this would only be an option in an emergency.

He had been financing a lifestyle he could not afford with military money and he knew they were starting to close in. Too many questions had been asked and two days ago they had wanted to see his records.

The machine had come at just the right time. He could have disappeared, but he did not want to spend his life on the run. That was no fun at all. It was him that did the hunting, somehow being prey did not sit well.

If they had not wanted him to take the money they should not have made it so easy for him to get it. 'Stupid,' he thought. It had been so simple, it was a joke. There was so much money passing through the military it was just waiting to be picked up. He was astounded it was noticed; maybe they were not as stupid as he thought. They could not say for sure, but they definitely suspected and it was just a matter of time before they found out.

Ten million was hard to conceal. That was the problem, there was just so much of it he could not spread it thin enough to completely hide it away.

He twitched his shoulders; maybe he should not have been so greedy. That thought hurt, he was not used to admitting to any fault.

Either way, it was definitely a good time to get out. He smiled. Besides, this was a lot more exciting than his day-to-day job. He had been so bored he could have died. That was what had started him off with the money. Initially it was to see if he could do it, then it was for the excitement and the lavish lifestyle did not hurt.

Excitement was what he craved. Life had been so dull, even in the army. He envied his counterpart. A professional killer, the report had said. He tightened his mouth and nodded. 'Now that's what I call impressive.' Still, he was more ambitious than simply being king of Alnwick and as a skilled engineer, he fully intended moving further afield once he assessed which soldiers would be the best to make up his own private army. As for the other Briggs, he had different plans for him.

A sign caught in the headlights shot past, but not too fast for Briggs to see he was nearing Alnwick. A short while later he saw the turn off and began to slow on the approach. He did not want to drive into the town in case the sound of the engine would alert the occupants to his arrival. Instead, he would arm himself and walk the rest of the way. He travelled the length of the slip road and pulled in.

Soundproofing was minimum inside the compartment. The jeep was built more for speed than comfort and the diesel engine had obviously masked the noise, but when he switched off the car the crackle of machine gunfire interlaced with screams and distant explosions wafted across the Northumberland hills, welcoming him to the ancient town of Alnwick.

Chapter Eleven

En-route to Ponteland

"Jessica and I had been married for five years on the 22nd June," Jason said, his breathing quickening as the slope progressively increased upwards. "We met at Newcastle University when we were both lecturing on mathematics." He stopped speaking for a moment. "I wonder where she is now," he said softly. "Do you think she exists in this timeline?" He looked over his shoulder at Sarah, who was trailing behind. "Do you think..?" He stopped walking and turned to face the woman. "What's wrong?"

She was bent over, her head down by her knees, several yards further down the road.

Jason hurried down the hill.

"I suddenly felt really woozy." She returned upright, her face still pale in the torch light. "I thought I was going to faint."

"When did you last eat?" Jason asked, concerned.

"Nearly two days ago."

"Two days," he said, shocked, inwardly cringing, furious with himself for being so thoughtless and inconsiderate. "Why didn't you say something? You should have told me you were hungry."

"We had to keep moving. We need to get this timeline fixed and every second we stop to rest or eat is another second that might take us closer to being stuck in this hell hole for ever."

"That's true." He lowered his rucksack to the ground. "But I do have some tinned food in this bag which could be eaten on the move and several chocolate bars retrieved from the bunker stores which would make a scrummy dessert you could carry."

Sarah nodded. "OK, that's an option."

"I can't have you flagging on me." He dropped his head for a moment as he dug in the bag then returned upright when he found what he was looking for. "Fish."

When her eyes filled with hungry desire, Jason smiled and drew back the lid. "I take it that's a yes."

They continued up the road at a slightly slower pace whilst Sarah ate.

"I can't get used to the silence," Jason said, as they cleared the brow of the hill and caught their first glimpse of the road ahead.

The clouds had completely cleared to reveal a splattering of stars which broke up the blackness of the sky just enough to stop it merging with the pitch landscape. Directly ahead Spica and Arcturus outshone their more modest, but no less spectacular, companions and, slightly left, a small portion of the hundred billion stars in the Milky Way, only visible as a hazy snaking cloud, formed the backdrop for a forest on the horizon.

Sarah finished chewing and swallowed. "Is your world quite noisy?" she asked, before her next mouthful of fish.

"Yes. There was always the background hum of cars, aeroplanes and the sounds of life in general." Jason looked at her. "Surely it was the same in your world?"

"I suppose." She stopped eating and thought a moment. "It has seemed very quiet since the war. The noises you've described are sounds you just take for granted. They blend into the background and you just shut them off. I like the quiet, but this is a little too quiet even for me."

"Was there any warning about the war?"

"There were rumblings, but nothing to indicate there was a nuclear war coming. It caught everyone off guard. No-one ever thought it would happen like that. The UN had moved in as peacekeepers after tensions between Bolonia and Serboria had resulted in Bolonia's capital city being bombed. Last we'd heard Serboria was refusing to relinquish control, then next thing we knew we were nuked. Since then I haven't seen so much as a vapour trail or picked up a radio signal, so I can only assume the Northern Hemisphere was devastated and it may even be global."

"I grew up in the Cold War and they said you could go from nothing, not even so much as a skirmish, to full-scale nuclear war in four days."

"The Cold War?"

"A period where there was a great deal of tension between the Eastern Block and the West. Apparently, we came close to nuclear war on a number of occasions, but thankfully there were people on both sides who warned the opposition when it was time to keep things calm so as not to aggravate those with the itchy trigger fingers. We had seen the effects of a nuclear bomb on a population so we knew using it in a war situation was out of the question. Besides, fallout does not recognise borders and will just go wherever the air currents take it. There are still people today, decades after the Second World War, who are suffering from genetic problems because of radiation."

"What else do you think would be different in our timelines?"

Jason thought a moment. "Technology was the biggest jump that came as a result of the Second World War. Rockets, jets and computers were developed during the war, to help the war. There was also a leap in medical advancements in areas such as skin grafts, blood transfusions, which were developed before the war, but refined out of necessity during the war, and large-scale immunisations against diseases like tetanus."

Sarah nodded, her attention focused on the tin as she cleaned the last of the meat from the container. "Everyone is immunised against a number of diseases as a child and we have jets and computers."

"But how sophisticated are they?"

She glanced at Jason. "What do you mean?"

"We have computers in just about everything. We have computers in our cars, our televisions and we have little handheld computers you can carry around with you."

She shook her head. "We have nothing like that. It's mostly businesses that use computers." She looked at Jason curiously. "How can you get a computer so small you can carry it in your hand? The smallest computer I've seen was the size of a desk."

"They have tiny printed circuitry, which replaced the large silicon motherboards and plug-in chips. How far has the space programme gone?"

She furrowed her brow. "Space programme?"

"Have they gone to the moon?"

"No. They sent a man to the edge of space, just to see if they could do it, but no further."

"The Americans launched nine Apollo missions, six of which landed on the moon."

"Really!" Sarah's eyes widened. "That's amazing."

"Since then there has been a joint international effort to permanently occupy space through the Space Station?"

She shook her head, bemused. "Space Station?"

"First there was MIR, a Russian-built space station, then when MIR started to get old, the international communities clubbed together to build the ISS, which is a permanently manned facility orbiting about two hundred and fifty miles above the Earth."

Sarah stared at Jason, engrossed. "We have nothing like that."

"You said you have jets, but have you achieved supersonic air travel?"

"The sound barrier was broken some time ago and the military jets can travel, I think, at Mach two."

"Is your supersonic flight limited to the military or do any of your commercial jets travel faster than sound?"

"No," Sarah said emphatically.

"We had a commercial jet called Concorde which could fly as fast as your military jets and could complete a transatlantic crossing in about three and a half hours."

"Wow! A flight to New York usually takes about nine hours and if you travel on one of the propeller planes, it can take anything up to twelve."

"What about computers? How developed are your computers?"

"Computers are used all the time in schools and in the workplace."

"Do you have touch screens?"

"I've heard of them," Sarah said cautiously, "but I think they are quite specialised. I noticed there was one on your time machine."

"Yes. In my timeline they're common. There are touch screens on home computers, in cars and on mobile phones."

Sarah had started on a second tin of fish. She stopped. "Mobile phones? What, do you mean cordless phones?"

"No." Jason laughed. "Phones you can take out with you and can be used to make a call remotely."

"Your timeline sounds rather different from mine," she said as they continued.

"My timeline is just more advanced than yours because of the Second World War, which never happened in your timeline of course."

"Because you killed Hitler before the war began."

"Yes. There is always a technological push during times of war. It's sad to think our best advancements take place when we are at our worst."

Sarah looked ahead. The pitch black on the road was all-encompassing except for the small circle of light emitting from the torch which brightened the way just enough to stop the pair from drifting into a ditch. "Based on your theory we should advance at least five hundred years after the devastation of this war, but I somehow don't think that's going to happen."

"No, neither do I," Jason said ominously, "in fact I think it will be quite the opposite."

Chapter Twelve

On the Outskirts of Alnwick, Northumberland

Briggs stepped out of the jeep and listened to the sound of gunfire coming from the ancient town ahead. It was hard to tell how many people were involved, but it was obviously a bit more than a fight between two small factions.

The gunfire was extensive and seemed to be spread over several areas of the town, although the exact location was not easy to identify as the surrounding hills created a bounce-back effect which confused the senses.

He had studied the layout of the town in detail and visited the library to investigate the location of all the windows, doors, fire exits and even vents, which could be used as entry points to prepare for his journey into the past. He was happy that he knew the town and particularly the library intimately – but he had not anticipated this.

He moved to the back of the vehicle and popped open the cover protecting the boot, flung it onto the roof and pressed the switch to illuminate the small LED light still attached to the metal frame inside the trunk. To the left of the boot was a large, dark olive, canvas kit bag, secured to the interior wall with tape.

Briggs pulled on the straps and the tiny hooks on the overlapping band, deeply imbedded into the fabric, made a distinct, unavoidable and rather loud hissing sound as they parted. This was not a problem under the circumstances and he released the first without incident, but as he pulled on the second strap, a break in the fighting made him look around nervously. It was apparent that the noise was obviously man-made and it may have travelled for some distance in the otherwise deathly silence of the post-apocalyptic world. He scanned the vicinity to check he was still alone before returning his attention to the task at hand.

In the distance, an explosion briefly lit up a cluster of rooftops on the far side of the town. For a moment, screams could be heard before they were drowned out when the firing started again.

Briggs lifted the bag from the trunk, placed it down on the road, opened the zip and started to remove some of the contents, placing them back into the boot so that he could see what he had.

A bulletproof vest was propped up against the spare tyre, secured to a frame running along the back of the seats. Next, a utility belt, which had compartments for several guns, hand grenades and an assortment of knives, was spread out to await its implements. Then he started with the weapons.

Two semi-automatics, one with a silencer attached, a handgun and two combat knives, one with a serrated blade and the other a double-edged dagger, were all placed into their housings before he slipped on the bulletproof vest and buckled up the belt. He returned to the bag, removed a pair of infrared goggles and slipped the strap over his head. Then finally, he retrieved the booklet lying on the back seat of the jeep and placed it into a pocket on the inside of the flack jacket.

A copy he made of Jason's report, in case the original was damaged, had been left in a pouch behind the driver's seat. He thought better of it and moved it to the boot, before securing the jeep and joining the road on foot.

The library was on the far side of town, so Briggs would have had to cross through the centre of Alnwick to reach the two-storey building. Ordinarily this would have been his chosen route, as it would have been the quickest way to reach the library, but the running battle taking place on the streets of Alnwick prompted a change of plan and he decided to adopt Jason's route into the town instead.

A brisk walk and ten minutes later he arrived at the edge of the forest. Once there he stopped. When he switched off the car headlights his eyes began adjusting to the surrounding darkness and by now the transition was complete. Although still gloomy, his eyes could amass enough light from the fields surrounding the forest to be able to safely negotiate the undulations and rabbit holes pitting the grasses and soils, but as he stood looking at the forest, a wall of black awaited him a few metres in.

He slipped a red night vision torch off his belt and stepped into the trees.

The forest floor was littered with debris. Leaves, slick with water, carpeted the ground several inches thick for as far as the beam allowed him to see. The effects of the nuclear blast, which destroyed the RAF base at Boulmer and damaged part of the town before setting it ablaze, was also apparent through the shattered bricks and tiles which were scattered in amongst the foliage.

Slowly, Briggs picked his way through the forest, the way ahead lit with the red night vision torch.

He was now glad he had explored every aspect of Jason's journey. Entering the town any other way would have been impossible without the risk of getting caught up in the fighting. He had followed the scientist's route and had passed through the forest a week ago and had recognised the path Jason had said he had taken to enter Alnwick from the A1 slip road.

It was mentioned in his report, he and Sarah had been passed by a lorry in the early hours of the morning as they made their way to Ponteland. Inside the lorry were a number of men, one of which was badly injured and as it passed by, Jason stated, he could see it was towing a trailer filled with guns and heavy artillery.

Briggs suspected that the men in the lorry had something to do with the fighting and that they were battling to remove the killer, and his men, from power. He snorted. It was obvious his counterpart could not maintain sufficient control of the people and had not enforced his authority vigorously enough. Once *he* took command he would crush any rebellion fiercely and would leave no doubt as to who was in charge.

He started down a bank. The way would have been slightly easier, as the foliage was spread further apart, but the covering of soot made the leaves and branches slick and the distance between the trees prevented him using them effectively to slow his descent. Despite this his thickly treaded army boots still provided some additional traction where leaves and mud were concerned and before long, Briggs arrived in the valley at the bottom of the hill without incident. Back on level ground, he picked up the pace.

He could easily identify the location of the town; a brief lull in the gunfire allowed screams to be heard coming from the east and a glow could be seen in the distance, through a thinning in the trees.

Briggs stayed deep in the forest. The library was in the northern region of Alnwick and he could remain in the trees right up to the road which practically led to the door.

Suddenly, a loud hiss, sounding alarmingly close, signalled the launch of a missile. Briggs looked around, briefly panicked, then dived for cover just as an explosion shook the ground when the rocket detonated on the edge of the forest.

A billowing cloud of burning fuel climbed high into the sky, like a mini atom bomb, when the petrol station exploded. Two more blasts followed in quick succession before the forest once again fell silent.

Briggs climbed to his feet. “Stupid bastards,” he muttered, “there’s going to be nothing left to take over at this rate.” He dusted himself down and continued towards the library.

The forest smelled differently to how it did when he visited it last week.

It was at a similar time of year, the buds were just beginning to show on the tips of the branches even though spring had not officially arrived and it was still bitingly cold. It had rained the night before, scrubbing the air clean, leaving a freshness rarely encountered closer to the city. As he stepped into the trees, the aroma of rotting leaves and an earthy pungent smell joined the fresh crispness of the start of dawn to produce a heady scent which jolted the senses like the shock of an ice bath.

In this world, in this time, the clean freshness was gone, replaced by the sickly smell of decay wafting over the forest and clinging to his clothes and skin like poisonous treacle.

Briggs turned left when he found his way blocked by a barrier of thick shrubbery. He quickly made his way around and was pleased to see the way ahead was easier when the trees began to open out and thin. As the barriers diminished and grass replaced protruding roots and barbed branches, which snaked through the undergrowth to grab and snare, his pace increased.

The more wide spread the trees, the more disgusting the smell, and Briggs had to keep pausing to spit when a build-up of stench seemed to coat his inner mouth. Then he saw a clearing up ahead and realised the cause.

Jason had described, in the report, a grisly find in the forest on the outskirts of town.

Briggs stepped beyond the trees, into the glen – and here it was. He moved around until he was upwind, as the smell was almost unbearable and made him want to retch. On the far side of the mound, he stopped and stared when the scent reduced to a bearable level.

The pile of bodies was almost as tall as him and was easily four times wider. He stepped closer, studying the horror in more detail. It was hard to see whether they had died from physical injuries or from a lethal dose of radiation as there had been an attempt to burn the bodies. The fire must have been abandoned before it managed to take a good hold, though, as the flames had extinguished long before they had completed their task. Since then decomposition had ravaged what remained, although not enough to prevent some form of identification. A woman still wore her wedding ring, a man was in a fine winter coat, an old lady was dressed in a hospital gown and a child had their school satchel still draped over one shoulder.

Suddenly, voices in the distance caught Briggs' attention. Quickly, he returned to the shelter of the trees and waited to see if they were coming his way.

There was an altercation taking place. He listened carefully and soon realised it was more one-sided than the other. Two men were having an exchange, one the aggressor and the other on the defence.

He began to move cautiously in the direction of the voices. A short while later, just beyond a barrier of trees separating the glen from the road, which ran through the moors between Alnwick and Rothbury, he spotted the perpetrators next to an army vehicle which was parked in a muddy lay-by.

Briggs drew closer, then lowered himself down near a rocky outcrop, which allowed a good view of the clearing up ahead whilst still keeping him well concealed.

There were four men wearing army uniforms standing over two male civilians bound at the hands and feet, who were on their knees.

This was the first opportunity for Briggs to see the style of uniform the soldiers were wearing in this timeline and he was delighted to see it was the same as the one he was wearing from the bunker. He smiled. Once he had identified the Briggs from this timeline and killed him, he would be able to take his place as commanding officer without the worry of not blending in.

Three of the soldiers were holding standard-issue army rifles in a relaxed, but ready position and the fourth appeared to be unarmed. He was the source of the aggression. He towered over the man closest to Briggs' position, snarling down at him.

"I'm going to ask you one more time," he said in a menacing tone, "where is the lorry with the weapons being hidden?" He turned away from the civilian and walked a few paces, before turning back to confront the man.

Briggs froze when for a moment he saw the interrogator's face. It was stranger than he thought, looking at his own features when it was not into a mirror. This was the man he was looking for, the Briggs from this timeline, and with a rush of delight he realised it was going to be easier to kill him than he had anticipated.

Carefully, he reached around and popped open the catch keeping the semi-automatic with the silencer attached in place and pulled the gun free of its housing. He lowered himself back down and prepared to fire.

Everyone in the clearing would have to be killed to get rid of any witnesses, but he would take out the soldiers first as the men on the ground were not going anywhere in a hurry.

"I'm losing my patience," the mercenary snarled.

Briggs slipped on his infrared goggles and took aim; he had a good head shot. He squeezed the trigger, there was a noise like a balloon had deflated rapidly, then he nearly screamed out.

At the last moment, when it was too late for the signal between his brain and finger to change, the mercenary had bent forward and grabbed the civilian on the ground by his lapels.

The soldier standing to the left of the officer took the force of the bullet instead and he hit the ground, completely unaware that he was even dead.

The mercenary stood, made a quick signal to the others; they spread out in three directions and seconds later they were gone, disappearing into the trees.

Chapter Thirteen

En-route to Ponteland

"What time is it?" Sarah asked.

Jason glanced at his watch. "Just after two."

She pulled her coat tighter in an attempt to close any gaps. "No wonder it's so cold."

"It'll be a while before the sun rises. We should arrive in Ponteland before then."

"How much further do we have to go?"

"About another five miles." Jason looked at her. "How are you holding up?"

Sarah sighed. "Fine," she said flatly.

He studied her more intently. "It doesn't sound like fine to me."

She pulled a pained face. "I've walked this route twice already. Once with you when we went to Ponteland and you sent me back to Germany, and the other time was to check on my family a few days after Newcastle was bombed. Every time I come this way..." she paused, her mouth tight for a moment, "it brings back the grief I felt when I realised any hope of my family still being alive was gone," she choked.

"Aah!" Jason nodded. "I'm not surprised. I thought you were getting more agitated the further we went."

"The memory's still really raw."

"I can't imagine it'll ever be anything other than raw." He returned his attention to the road. "You never really recover from anything like that," he said softly, "especially when you're fighting for what's left of your life at the same time."

Suddenly, a loud shriek came from a field across the road.

Sarah stopped abruptly. "What's that?" she whispered.

Jason stood staring hopelessly into the darkness, unable to see anything other than black. "It sounds like a fox to me," he said confidently.

"Oh." She turned away from the field and carried on walking. "You're probably right."

"It's good to know other animals have survived."

"Yes, it is, as long as we don't end up on the menu."

Jason laughed. "There's something else I've noticed apart from the silence," he said.

"What's that?"

"The air quality."

"Are you talking about the smell?"

"Yes."

"That's because of the bomb."

"Because of the dust kicked up by the explosion?"

"No."

Jason looked at her, surprised. "But surely..."

She shook her head emphatically. "No," she snapped. "It is to some extent," she added more calmly, "but it's mostly because of the dead."

"What? Those who died from the radiation?" He glanced at the edge of the road where a grassy embankment lined the tarmac. "I saw one of those on my way to Morpeth. There was a young man sitting on the grass. He looked like he'd gotten too tired and had sat down and died. He had a rucksack and tent on his back like he was planning a long journey, but radiation sickness had obviously caught up with him quite early on." An overwhelming urge made Jason look around when he suddenly felt like they were being watched. "Mind you, I suppose it depends where he started as to whether it was early on or not. It may well have happened over a few days."

"There'll be plenty who have died since the blast," Sarah said ominously. She dipped her head left. "I mean, you wouldn't want to look too closely at those fields. At sun up you'll see they're full of dead animals. If that fox is after a meal there, it may be better off starving than eating radioactive meat. No, I don't think the smell is caused by those who have died since the blast, but by those who died in the blast. I think the smell is caused by the millions of bodies, vaporised and blasted up where they became a part of the very air itself."

Jason grimaced. "What a horrible thought," he said quietly.

"It materialised immediately after the bomb was dropped. I thought at first it was caused by the fires, but they only raged for a couple of days. No, it must be the smell of death, not just here on the ground, but everywhere; all around us."

Jason stepped in front of her and stopped walking.

"What's wrong?"

"I've suddenly remembered about a problem up ahead." He checked their location. "Now would be a good time to make a decision." He stabbed his thumb up the road. "We're nearing the Cramlington turn-off. We could leave the motorway now and take the road through Blagdon to get to Ponteland that way, or we can continue on this route and negotiate a scene that'll give me nightmares for the rest of my life."

"What was it?" Sarah asked, her eyes wide and staring.

“Not all the killing was as a result of the bomb. Someone must have decided to restrict the movement of people during a mass evacuation and they blocked the road with tanks. Some of the drivers must have tried to force their way through as there had been a shootout and there were a number of people, including soldiers, dead from gunshot wounds. At some point some of the cars must have crashed into the blockade and exploded. The heat from the fire must have been so intense it seemed to have melted the metal.” He turned to the south. “I’ve no doubt some of the stench we’re smelling is coming from there as all of the bodies were left where they died. The big question now is, does the Blagdon road even exist? I found out pretty quick not all of the roads in this timeline are the same as they are in mine.”

“Yes, it does.”

“And it’ll take us to Ponteland?”

“Yes.” She gave a slight shake, her body trembling. “I don’t wanna see the blockade, in case…” she seemed to hiccup as her words caught in her throat. She took a deep breath. “In case there is someone there I know.”

Jason tightened his mouth. “I agree. I think it would be a very bad idea. Come on.” He continued walking. “We should reach the turn-off in the next five minutes. It would be a better route to take in any case as it should hopefully get us there faster.”

Chapter Fourteen

On the Outskirts of Alnwick, Northumberland

Briggs stayed low, scanning for movement and heat signals in the surrounding forest. On his right there was a heat source spilling out from around a tree, but there were bushes and branches in the way and he could not guarantee getting a clean shot. He could not afford to only wound his victims as each shot had to count if he was to risk drawing attention to himself. Either way, he suspected this was the younger of the two surviving soldiers with the mercenary, as he could also hear movement from the same location, indicating a lack of experience in the field. He was fully aware of the man's location, but at this stage could not do anything about it.

****

Corporal John Rice tried to step around to look behind the tree. He stopped and physically cringed as the leaves crunched, yet again, beneath his boot. He lifted his foot and returned it to the base of the trunk, then cursed, muttering under his breath, when he caused another rustle.

Slowly, he turned, embracing the tree to steady himself, then snaked around and peered towards the location of the shot. He froze and focused, trying to blend in with the forest, but found all he could see was varying shades of black.

He tried to make out some form, anything that resembled a person, but could see nothing large enough to comprise a human being.

He was surprised that a silencer had been used; they were very expensive, as all relatively new inventions were. They would not be available to your average soldier and would more likely be used by a specialised division like the Special Forces, or a sniper. He understood from Sergeant Andrews that the weapons stored beneath the moor were there for emergency use in case of an invasion. He took this to mean it would not contain any specialist equipment, so this was an anomaly.

He moved back until he was again hidden by the tree. Well, hidden he hoped, as he did not have a clue as to where the gunman was.

A wave of sadness came over him and he took a deep hiccupping breath as he struggled to stop the swell of emotion that seemed to suddenly come from nowhere.

His family lived in Newcastle, just off the city centre. His dad had died two years ago in a road traffic accident and the moment he learned of the nuclear strike on the city, he accepted that the rest of his family were dead as well. His sister, two brothers and his mum would not have stood a chance.

He had learned all about the effects of nuclear weapons during his training and knew there was no hope unless you were in a bunker and even then, if it was a ground blast, survival there was still dubious.

He had accepted their deaths, but had not had the chance to mourn them. There had not been the time and even weeks later he knew he was still in shock. It was ongoing, there was no letting up. The nuclear attack, not just on the city, but on their army base at Otterburn, had resulted in the death of a number of friends who had stayed behind because they were not on the rota for the march out that day. The death of their captain soon after they moved into Alnwick, the dark changes in Sergeant Andrews' behaviour, Briggs taking control, the brutal ravaging of the town and its people under the guise of support. How could he recover when it had all turned to hell?

He attempted, too late, to suppress the emotions and the tears began to fall as all of his sorrow expanded, then brimmed over in a wave of uncontrollable grief. He lowered himself to the ground, sliding down the trunk, his face in his hand, and began to silently sob. No matter what happened here, if he survived, he had to get out of this place and away from the monster that was now running this unit, otherwise he knew he would be siding with the civilians before long, like some of his other colleagues did when the fighting started.

****

Sergeant William Andrews slowly stood and wiped his hands down his thighs. He was searching for the gunman and had guessed why they had been so accurate when firing in the blackness of the forest at night. He needed his body to cool down so he could hide his heat from the thermal camera he suspected the shooter was wearing. He wiped the last of the mud on his hands over his face for good measure, then continued in the direction indicated by his commanding officer.

Andrews always liked the mercenary even many years ago when they were in the same unit together. He was exciting and had a killer edge, which was obvious even in peace times. He was not surprised to find him standing there with three dead men at his feet, when they met again on the streets of Alnwick, days after the nuclear attack plunged mankind back to the dark ages.

Andrews was sure the mercenary was responsible for killing Captain Harrison, but no-one ever talked about it and he was not going to confront him on the subject, as it would be extremely dangerous. There were limits to their friendship. He had not tested the boundaries and never would, as he did not want to personally find out how sophisticated a killer this man truly was.

Harrison was a good man and Andrews enjoyed working under his command, but these were different times requiring a different approach; a more ruthless type of leadership was needed otherwise none of them were going to survive. Given the choice he would have rather the two had worked together as Harrison would have added a compassionate side to the mercenary's hard, calculating edge and he had no doubt the situation they were having to deal with on the streets of Alnwick now would have never happened. Either way, even if Harrison had not been killed, it would not have worked, he knew the mercenary's sort and sharing the leadership was not his style.

Andrews knew his place, at the mercenary's right hand and no more. He did as he was told and that was that. At least that is what he could tell himself in the dark days of the nightmares, if they ever returned to normal civility.

****

Briggs scanned the forest for any heat sources. He had good flexibility and although he could not quite see all around, he had enough of a view to feel comfortable that he would find all three of them soon.

He could no longer see the young soldier, but knew where he was from the sound of his sobbing. It was obvious he was trying to stifle his grief, but had not succeeded enough to suppress all noise. It was very subtle, but intermittent gasps could be heard when there was a break in the gunfire. Still, he was not visible and did not offer himself up as a viable target.

The other two he had lost entirely. He was not too worried about the other soldier, but the mercenary was a different matter. He would have been a lot happier if he had been able to keep a track on him. Even if he could not get a shot, Briggs would have felt more comfortable if he was aware of his location. Still, he was confident no-one was going anywhere without his say so; he was certain of that.

He checked the younger soldier and found all he could see was his foot and the lower part of his calf, just above the line of his boot. It was not worth revealing his hiding place for a shot that would do nothing more than reduce his mobility. If necessary, he would take it to stop him running away, but only if he managed to kill the other two first.

He looked left. There were heat sources passing along the forest floor, moving between the branches and leaves, and were more than likely scavengers living off the dead that had fallen because of the bomb.

He shifted onto his elbow to get a better look around and an indistinct movement caught his attention. He stopped, completely rigid, and looked for a heat source.

A faint glow, that was already fading, was hovering in the air. At first, Briggs was confused and could not identify the origin, until the warm orange orb, with a dark centre, moved and it dawned on him it was the barrel of a gun. The weapon had obviously recently been fired and the residual heat could still be detected by his thermal goggles.

He was surprised he was not picking up any heat from the carrier of the weapon and it was only when they moved that he was alerted to their presence. He froze when suddenly they turned and looked at him.

The camouflage covered every part of the man's body except his eyes, which glowed an eerie red, as they could not be masked by any cooling effect.

Slowly, Briggs lifted his gun and aimed. He did not want to have to shoot him, not at this stage at least. He would only fire if his life was in immediate danger.

The man stood rigid, then slowly he swung his gun around and pointed it directly at Briggs.

This was the move Briggs was primed for. He fingered the trigger and was just about to fire, when the man shifted his line of focus and lowered his weapon.

Briggs kept his attention fixed on the soldier in case he became a threat again, but lowered his level of alert by moving his finger off the trigger. Suddenly, his eyes shot wider and his heart rate jumped when a barely detectable noise came from behind. Years of training came into play and in less than a second his muscles tightened in preparation to roll and fire – but it was already too late when a sharp sting, felt briefly at the base of his skull, was the only indication he had of the ambush that had been taking place in the forest behind.

****

The mercenary pushed the blade upward, driving it deep beneath the man's skull, then as his body went limp, moved it around to make sure he completed the kill.

Chapter Fifteen

Outskirts of Ponteland, Northumberland

"Wow! Look at that."

Jason jumped. The pair had walked in silence for the past hour and he had almost forgotten Sarah was there. He had drifted into his own quiet world, as he often did when he was upset, where he brooded and festered on his problems until he either came up with a solution or dug himself into a deep pit of depression. The strain of this world was dragging him down and he had only been here just over three days. He could not imagine how bad it had been for Sarah, least of all how she kept going every day.

Most of their journey had taken place through the night in darkness surrounded by shapes coloured in various shades of greys and blacks with very little definition to give them anything other than form, but now the sun had begun to rise and the blackness had started to lift. It was not above the horizon yet, as dawn had only just started, but the sky had already shifted from an inky black to a sapphire blue. It was enough to allow other colours to join the brightening of the ether and to bring the shadowy world of night back into the assorted colours of day.

Jason looked around in the direction Sarah had indicated.

They were passing the airport and could see the runway over the tops of the hedges, separating a grassy verge edging the road from the airfield's grounds. In their line of sight should have been the control tower, normally looming behind the main airport building, but the circular pad was caught up in the shockwave from the blast and had severed from the supporting column, killing everyone inside when it plunged twelve metres onto the concrete below.

Jason stopped and stared for a moment, taking in the sight.

At ground zero, the heat from the bomb reached temperatures of millions of degrees centigrade, enough to vaporise everything within a mile of the impact site, but it quickly diminished. By the time it reached the airport it was only sufficient to produce first-degree burns on exposed skin and to ignite anything flammable.

A jumbo jet, fully loaded with fuel, was hit by the shockwave as it taxied for take-off. The side impact had tumbled the plane onto the left wing, which cracked on impact with the ground, released fuel, stored in chambers within the appendage, and ignited on the burning grass. The resulting explosion ripped the plane into three pieces and the ensuing firestorm gutted the carcass and left a charred shell upended and buried in the soil on the far side of the hedge.

"Do you think there was anyone inside?" Jason asked, unable to tear his eyes away from the carnage.

"Probably." Sarah turned away from the scene and dropped her head. "It all happened so fast, there was very little warning. Everyone was just going about their business as usual. We knew there were tensions brewing between Serboria and Bolonia, but nobody expected it to lead to global nuclear war." She started walking again. "I don't know whether anything happened in the city, but we never heard any air raid sirens out in Morpeth."

Jason stood a moment longer before he followed Sarah, trailing slightly behind.

Half an hour later they arrived on the main high street running through the centre of Ponteland.

"That's incredible," Jason gasped.

Sarah looked around and after a few seconds, gave up trying to see the 'incredible' Jason was talking about. "What?"

"That sunrise."

She looked ahead at the fiery oranges merging into rose and crimson and the wispy clouds edged with mauve greeting the rising sun. "You get used to it," she said flatly. "It's caused by the nuclear fallout; you know, like after a volcano erupts." She looked at him and wrinkled her nose, her cheeks rising to chubby mounds beneath her eyes. "Sort of spoils it a bit, doesn't it?"

Jason glanced at her uncomfortably. "Yes, it does."

"I'm just running on adrenaline now," she warned. "I'm not sure I dare sit down." Her mouth twitched into a smile. "I'm sure I'd fall asleep."

"Well, you'll be glad to know we haven't got much further to go." He looked over his shoulder to check they were not being followed.

Sarah looked at him sideways. "What's the matter? You seem edgy."

"I can't get used to the streets being so empty. It was strange in Morpeth and along the motorway, but here, because it's my home, you know," Jason shrugged his shoulders, "somewhere you're supposed to feel safe, it's just so creepy. I can appreciate what they mean by ghost town."

Sarah tipped her head back, flexing her neck. "I'm having trouble remembering that we haven't done this before." She returned her attention to Jason. "You should be glad; the last time we were here together we were shot at several times."

Jason laughed nervously. "Suppose I should. Not too keen on that." He pointed to a road ahead. "We need to go down that street."

Sarah scanned the rows of houses, looking for any sign of life.

There were very few windows with their curtains closed, as the attack happened in the late afternoon when the majority of people were still at work. This allowed a glimpse of the empty rooms beyond, still pristine enough to offer a false sense of normality.

"What's your house number?" she asked.

"Sixty-three." Jason thought a moment, then, "Except it's not my house any more."

She looked at him, puzzled. "It must be your house; the machine is there."

"Well, no. The machine is protected from the effects of time, otherwise it would not be there when I needed to come back. There are probably parts on that machine which don't exist in this timeline. Materials that haven't been invented yet like nano-carbon technology, which was groundbreaking in my timeline, but when you're twenty or thirty years behind, there's no way it would be available here. It has to protect itself from the effects of time, otherwise it could cease to function or possibly even exist. Besides, I know it's not my house because the decor and furniture were completely different. The machine was about the only consistent thing there. Outside of the basement the layout of the house was the same, but everything else was wrong."

"Was the house empty?"

"Yes."

"Do you think the owners were out?"

"No, it was five in the morning and judging by the water, leaf litter and gathering mould at the front door, I don't think it had been occupied for some time. Also, upstairs there were clothes scattered and drawers left open as though someone had packed in a hurry."

"There was a lot of panic, as you can imagine, immediately after we were attacked. I never saw what happened closer to the city, but I would have thought it was far worse than what happened at Morpeth. People just wanted to get as far away from the bomb as possible. Within a few hours it felt like the whole of Morpeth had emptied."

"It must have been terrible."

Sarah simply nodded.

Jason nudged his head. "It's the next house up."

Chapter Sixteen

On the Outskirts of Alnwick, Northumberland

Andrews trotted up as the mercenary pulled the knife clear of the man's skull. A thick flow of blood oozed from the cavity along with the extracted blade, soaked the hair at the base of his scalp, then trickled down his neck to pool on the ground beneath the body.

"I'd just found him," Andrews informed his commander breathlessly. "I could barely see him. I only spotted him because of the undergrowth. It suddenly looked particularly dense in the middle, then I saw a flash of flesh when he moved his hand. I would've taken him down, but I saw you coming up behind."

Andrews had recently noticed he had been getting breathless very easily and swore he could feel the damage the radiation was doing to his lungs. This was confirmed by a doctor, on a visit to the local hospital, who simply nodded when directly asked by the officer if this was the case.

A handful of nurses and two doctors were trying to keep a service going in the small community hospital against the odds. The population of Alnwick had tripled over the last few weeks once word got around that the army had set up a food distribution programme and a number of those coming into the town were already ill from the fallout. They required specialised treatment, which would usually involve them being transferred to a major hospital closer to Newcastle, but a small group, who had travelled on a reconnaissance to gather medical supplies, reported back only one of those hospitals still remained standing and had been abandoned due to its proximity to the city.

Briggs bent forward and examined the body at his feet. "I knew roughly where he was from the angle of the shot and from the direction that Mendeck's body fell. It was unlikely he was going anywhere, so we just had to be quick." Briggs wiped the blade clean on the shooter's jacket and returned it to its housing before he retrieved a torch and shone it down on his victim's body. "He's pretty well equipped for a townsperson." He looked at Andrews. "Maybe we've got something different here."

Andrews shrugged, the corners of his mouth turning down. "It could be equipment they found in the Town Moor bunker."

Suddenly, an explosion that lit up the edge of the forest caused Briggs to snap upright. He looked towards the town. As the rumble died screams could be heard, followed by voices calling out for an immediate surrender.

He returned his attention to the body, lowered himself down onto his haunches and fingered the strap, keeping the night vision goggles in place. "It's unlikely these were found in the bunker," he said distantly, "they're too specialised. There would have been a store of food and weapons, but night vision goggles are relatively new technology." He moved his thumb beneath the strap and shifted it up and over the man's head, then grabbed the shooter's left shoulder. "Let's see what we've got." He turned the body over onto its back in a single movement, then stood upright, shocked.

"What the hell?" Andrews squawked. He reached down, pulled the goggles completely free of the head and laughed nervously. "He looks exactly like you."

Briggs stared into the gaping eyes of the cadaver, still wide in the alarm that was felt seconds before the point of death, when the shooter realised he had not been the hunter after all, but was in fact the prey. "I think if this man had been running around the town, we would have most certainly noticed him."

Andrews snorted. "Yeah."

"He must be from outside."

Andrews' face furrowed, he shook his head. "The resemblance is uncanny."

"Check him for ID."

The sergeant dropped to his knees and rummaged through the shooter's pockets.

Briggs waited. A short while later Andrews had collected a small bundle of items.

Briggs passed him the torch then examined the pile. "A key." He looked at the fob. "Army jeep. KBF TA," he said curiously.

"Kenton Bank Foot Territorial Army," Andrews prompted.

"Oh, yeah. A..." he paused, his face furrowed. "I don't know what this is..." He handed the microchip embedded in the small circuit board back to the officer.

He examined it from all angles. "I've never seen anything like it," he confessed.

"Put it somewhere safe, just in case." The final item was opened out until it was spread wide, "And a wallet." He searched through the contents. "Some money. Do you recognise this?"

Andrews looked at the coins. "It's British, but we have pound notes, not coins," he said curiously.

"A credit card." Briggs slipped the small card out from the clear plastic internal pocket and held it under the torch. He examined the name. "I R Briggs," he said slowly. The two men looked at each other.

"This is getting way too creepy," Andrews said, his face ashen in the spread of the beam. "That's your name, Ian Robert Briggs."

Briggs looked at the keys. "If we find that vehicle, and it must be close by, I'll bet we'll get a better idea of where this little bastard came from. In the meantime," he bent forward and removed the gun from his double's dead hand, "I'll have this." He smiled. "A silencer is always useful."

Chapter Seventeen

Ponteland, Northumberland

Jason turned to enter the gate leading to his house and immediately stopped.

"What's wrong?" Sarah asked.

He turned his head so he could speak to her more quietly. "The front door was open and now it's closed."

"Could it have blown shut?"

"Unlikely, there was a lot of debris jamming it open."

He gently depressed the catch and slowly pushed the gate open to avoid making a noise. He stepped onto the path and cautiously made his way to the door.

Sarah followed, quietly closing the gate behind.

He stopped at the door and gave it a firm push. "Did this happen before?" he asked, when it refused to budge.

"No, but we are now running on a later timescale," she replied, hushed.

He looked at her curiously. "What do you mean?"

Sarah's face furrowed. "What day are we on?" She shook her head. "I'm losing track. Either way, the two days you took to get back to the bunker at Kenton Bank Foot was the entire time period you spent in this timeline last time. At this point, we've added at least twenty-four hours onto that timeline already with our journey to and from Morpeth."

"Oh, yes, I see," Jason said, when she finished. He stepped up to a front window and cupped his hands against the glass. "So this might have happened, but when you did this before you arrived at the house the equivalent of yesterday."

"Yes."

The room was shrouded in gloom despite the morning light.

"I can't see anyone," Jason reported, "but there could be someone lying on the couch. It's just out of sight. All I can see is an arm rest."

"Could we get in through the back?"

"It's worth a shot." He moved away from the window and followed Sarah to the side gate, then around to the garden at the rear of the house. He stepped up to the door and tried the handle, but was again disappointed to discover it was locked.

Sarah moved up to the kitchen window and looked in. "I can see a key lying on the bench." She stepped away from the sill and crossed to some bedding plants in a border nearby.

Most of the flora in the garden was bare, an apparent testament to the grip winter still held on the Northern Hemisphere. However, the evergreens told a more sinister story, reflecting the real events now shaping the world. Withered leaves were not curled as though desiccated, but unfurled, brown and blackened where they had been burnt around the edges. Not quickly, as they would have been if they had been caught up in the fireball, but slowly over a number of weeks. Even the hardy conifers had not survived. Toxic dust washed out of the air by snow settled on the branches and poisoned the foliage and soil at the base of the trees.

Sarah stooped and picked up an ornamental rock below a shrivelled rose bush on the edge of the grass. She turned and, before Jason could stop her, hurled it through the glass embedded in the back door.

The scientist turned on her furiously. "What did you do that for? Why the hell are we trying to be quiet if you're going to do something stupid like that?"

Sarah ignored him, stepped up to the door and reached in through the broken glass. "You wanted to know if anyone was in the house." She grabbed the key off the bench and inserted it into the lock. "Well, that'll certainly bring them running." She smiled at Jason when there was a distinct click, opened the door and stepped into the kitchen. "We do not have the time to mess around," she said firmly as the scientist followed her behind. "Until we take control of the other machine we are completely at the mercy of Briggs. He could choose to go back to the bunker and destroy it at any point. We would then be left trying to get a hold of a generator so that we could get this machine working instead."

"Yes, of course. You're absolutely right," Jason said, more subdued, "sorry." He walked past Sarah and started through the kitchen and into the hall.

"And as nobody has come running," she pointed out, "it looks like the house is empty and the front door just happened to close on its own."

The pair stopped abruptly when a male voice said, "Wrong on both accounts."

Chapter Eighteen

Alnwick, Northumberland

Briggs looked around the trees, trying to get his bearings. "Right," he said, "where did we leave those guys? They're going to tell me what they've done with the weapons."

The two officers went rigid and looked sharply right when the sound of running through the undergrowth interrupted the silence that had returned to the forest since the fighting had stopped.

Corporal John Rice watched Briggs kill the shooter and realised how close he had come to being killed himself, as he was well within the man's line of vision. If he had not been hidden by the tree, he realised, he would now be dead. This, he decided, was too much and a sign he had to get away from this place. Nothing else mattered. He would never be able to rebuild a life with these people. He had to go. He watched and waited until the two officers were distracted, then decided to run. At first, the fighting covered his escape, but an unexpected cessation in hostilities allowed his heavy-footed dash to be heard for some distance around.

Briggs picked up the night vision goggles from beside the body at his feet and slipped them on. He looked towards the sound and quickly found a heat source hurrying through the trees. "It's Corporal Rice," he said. He raised the gun with the silencer attached and prepared to fire.

Andrews reached out and touched the hand holding the weapon. "No. Let him go."

Briggs looked at the sergeant, the cooling effect of the mud still masking his body heat so only his eyes glowed red within the scopes. "You're not getting soft on me, are you?" he said, his scowl hidden behind the binocular-style goggles.

"No. I'm sick of having to tell him everything at least twice. He can't follow a command without me having to remind him about what I told him to do a few minutes earlier and even then he sometimes has to be told again. It's classic battle fatigue. He's washed out. He's no longer good for duty. I just don't see the need to kill him."

Briggs lowered the gun. "OK. I just better not see him around here ever again," he yelled, towards the sound of the man running, "or I'll not be so compassionate next time and he'll definitely wind up dead." He slipped off the night vision goggles. "Come on," he said to Andrews, "let's finish our interrogation."

The two men were several yards apart by the time the officers returned to the clearing. Neither one of them were where they had been left. Both had been trying to crawl on their knees, their hands still tied behind their backs, their feet still bound at the ankles, in an attempt to escape.

Briggs strode up to the nearest. He grabbed the man by his hair and pulled his head back, causing him to grimace in pain.

"Where are the weapons?" he snarled in his face.

"I don't know," the man howled.

"I don't believe you. You were sent to gather food from the bunker beneath the Town Moor and came back with weapons, and you are now telling me that you don't know who has them." He stood and shot the man's colleague, who was cowering on his knees a short distance away.

For a few seconds the man jerked violently on the ground until Briggs pumped another bullet into the body.

He returned his attention to the man at his feet. "Now, one more time. Where are the weapons?"

"Fuck yo..."

Briggs killed him before he finished his curse, shoved the body away when it landed across his foot, then sighed. "Well, it has gone quiet." He looked through the trees. "Let's hope the men have found the stash of weapons and taken back the town."

A short while later the captain strode into the library with Andrews following close behind. “Well done,” he said to the small group of soldiers in the room. “Where are the rebels being held?” he asked.

“In the basement,” Corporal Richard Aston replied. He was nursing a bullet wound to his right arm. It was wrapped in a makeshift bandage, prepared from a small towel, cut into strips. It had already bled through and did not appear to be stopping as the crimson circle continued to expand.

“How many are there?” Briggs asked.

“Ten.”

“And have you retrieved the weapons?”

“Yes.”

“Excellent.” The mercenary flashed a rare smile. “I want those involved executed.” He started to turn away then stopped when for a moment the corporal looked shocked. Briggs’ face darkened, the smile forgotten. “Do you have a problem with that?” he challenged.

Richard flushed, he shook his head. “No! It’s just I thought if we took back the weapons,” he flustered, “and punished them by reducing their food rations for a month, that could be enough.”

Briggs moved up to the solider until they were almost touching. “Enough for what? Enough to make them just fall into line. Enough to stop them launching an attack in the middle of the night when you’re sleeping.” He stepped back and spoke to the rest of the platoon. “I want you to go door to door. Everyone is to be told they are to gather in the town square tomorrow at eight to witness the executions and I want them told that if there are any more uprisings, it won’t just be them, but two of their family members that will die alongside them next time. Move!” He turned to Andrews. “In the meantime we’ll start a search for that army vehicle.”

“Sir. Are you looking for an army vehicle that doesn’t belong to us?”

Briggs stopped and looked at the Private. "Yes, do you know anything? Have you seen a strange vehicle in or around the town?"

"Yes, sir. When we were circling around the rebels we came across a jeep just off Willowburn Avenue. We thought it might have been commandeered by the rebels as none of us recognised the plates. We refrained from breaking in as there was nothing spectacular about it and we thought it would just be an unnecessary waste of time."

"OK. You go with the rest of the platoon and Sergeant Andrews and I will check it out."

Briggs floored the accelerator and sped through the town of Alnwick. He knew they should be walking as fuel was almost as valuable as food these days and it would not be long before they would have to move further afield if they wanted to keep their vehicles moving. Come the spring, when it would be essential to sow crops, fuel for tractors would become a priority, unless they wanted to go back to using a horse and plough. Still, despite this he had a really bad feeling about this man and wanted to examine the jeep as fast as possible.

Evidence of the fighting could be seen all throughout the town. Bullet holes peppered the ancient town walls and a large crater in the road, surrounded by debris, forced Briggs to slow and negotiate a safe route around. A number of civilians were being treated for their injuries at the side of the road and a couple of men were lying, unmoving, face down a short way from the town gates. A smell of gunpowder lingered in the air as they drove past several empty shells, but the scent quickly dissipated as they moved into streets unaffected by the battle.

Soon the vehicle left the main hub of the town behind and headed south into the suburbs.

Andrews pointed as they rounded a bend and got a clear view of the road ahead. "There it is."

Briggs accelerated then pulled up sharply, skidding slightly on the frosty road before coming to a halt alongside the abandoned jeep. He stepped onto the tarmac, retrieved the key from his jacket pocket, inserted it into the lock and gave a slight smile when he heard a click as the door unlocked. He opened it wide, slid into the driver's seat and searched the glove compartment.

In the meantime, Andrews examined the back seat of the vehicle before moving to the boot and popping the cover. "You're gonna wanna come see this," he called.

Briggs returned to the road and joined his second-in-command at the rear of the jeep.

"Most impressive," Andrews laughed. "He obviously meant business." He pushed the weapons case off to one side to give it room to open out fully, then stopped. "What's this?" He picked up an A4 booklet bound in red webbing and handed it to Briggs.

Chapter Nineteen

Ponteland, Northumberland

Jason and Sarah froze and stared at the young man pointing the gun directly at them.

It was hard to gauge his age as the debilitating and destructive effects of the radiation on his skin had left it covered in open sores, sallow, and had left his face sunken through a loss of teeth and borderline starvation. Evidence of malnourishment was supported by his clothes, which drooped and hung from his body as though they were at least a size too big.

Jason glanced over his shoulder. “I told you we should have been more discreet,” he hissed.

“Why more discreet?” the young woman standing behind the gunman challenged. “What were you going to do? Kill us?”

She seemed to be fairing little better than her partner and her short cropped blonde hair was thinning and patchy in places.

“No, of course not,” Jason snapped. “There’s something I need in this house. I was just coming to get it.”

“This is our house,” the man snarled.

“You can keep the house, I don’t want the house. I just need something from the basement,” Jason urged. He took a step forward, then raised his hands quickly and froze again when the man became more agitated.

“Stay where you are,” he screamed, waving the shotgun in Jason’s face. “You don’t move unless I say.”

Sarah leaned around to engage with the pair. “We have clean food.” She knew she had said the right thing when they suddenly locked eyes with her.

“Clean, as in not contaminated?” the woman questioned cautiously.

“Yes.”

"There's no such thing," the man snorted. "It'll be just as toxic as everything else. We were forced to come back here because there are too many people moving north and just about everything has been raided. There's only the food closer to the city left and it's all contaminated. We had to take our chances or starve."

The woman moved nearer to her partner. "They might be telling the truth," she said, her voice hushed.

"We are telling the truth," Jason stated. "It was protected."

She stepped around from behind the man. "Do you have clean water as well?" she asked, her eyes abnormally large.

"Protected? Where?" the man interrupted before Jason had the chance to respond.

"It was in a bunker in Kenton," Jason replied, "and yes, we do have clean water."

The gunman pointed at Sarah. "I can see she's looking a bit ropey, but you... Were you in the bunker or something? You're the healthiest person I've seen in a while."

"I think we've told you enough," Sarah snapped. "We'll give you the food and water in exchange for access to the basement, then we'll leave you alone in the house."

The man stood rigid, holding himself upright. "My thinking is that we'll take the food and water and keep whatever is so important in the basement as well. It might be good to trade."

Jason was regretting packing his gun and not carrying it constantly where it could be easily accessed. The incident in Germany which caused the horrific time split had made him reluctant to ever touch a gun again, but still, the damage was done, and to be blasé about his personal protection he now knew was at best stupid and at worst dangerous. "What's in the basement is no good to you. It's valuable only to me and nobody else. I'll take you down and show you." He pointed at the door.

The young man involuntarily looked in the indicated direction, giving Jason the time to grab the barrel of the gun. Immediately, he turned it off to one side, to make sure it was away from Sarah, and stepped forward to punch the attacker firmly on the jaw.

One of the barrels fired in the process and for a moment drowned out the screams of fury from his companion.

The man, weakened from a lack of food, lurched slightly under the force of the blow. Still, he had at least ten years' youth on his side and was stronger than Jason anticipated. He firmed his grip on the gun and the two began to wrestle. Twisting and turning, they stood chest to chest, their arms locked, each trying to gain some ground over the other.

The woman moved back to give her partner room and was goading him on with increasing zeal the more she sensed victory.

The man's desperation made him strong and he soon forced the scientist against the wall.

Jason struggled to keep control of the gun for fear the second barrel would discharge into Sarah. "We don't have to do this," he said through gritted teeth. "I only want what's in the basement." There was movement out of the corner of his eye and he glanced sideways to find Sarah was gone.

"You're not taking our stuff," the man snarled. "Everything in this street is ours."

In the kitchen, Sarah quickly searched drawers and cupboards for a weapon. She glanced around to see how Jason was doing and found the young woman blocking the doorway. She returned to her task, ignoring the imminent danger, and was relieved to find that the next drawer she opened contained a knife. She removed it, turned and threatened the woman.

"You better know how to use that," she sneered confidently, moving closer.

Sarah dipped the weapon. "Maybe I don't know how to use that, but I do know how to use this." She stepped up, closing the gap, moved a can of air freshener out from behind her back and depressed the button directly at the woman's eyes.

She screamed and flung her hands over her face, stumbling backwards, to evade the attack.

This was the distraction the scientist needed as the man caught off guard by his companion's cries loosened his grip on the weapon enough for Jason to fling him off and push him to the ground before turning the gun around to keep him at bay. "Stay down!" he ordered. "Sarah, are you all right?"

"Yes, everything's under control," she called.

The young woman had fallen backwards and was sitting howling on the kitchen floor, her face cradled in her hands.

Sarah put down the spray, lowered her backpack and opened the zipper.

The woman looked up as she stepped closer. Her eyes, red and swollen, were watering profusely.

"You make one wrong move and I'll kill you," Sarah warned. She unscrewed a bottle of water retrieved from her bag and poured some of the contents gently into the woman's eyes.

She blinked rapidly several times before squeezing her lids tightly shut, then lowering her head and carefully rubbing them to help the cleaning process. "Thank you," she said hesitantly.

Sarah helped her up then bustled her forward to join her companion.

"Sit down," Jason ordered. He waited for her to comply, before asking Sarah, "Can you get the semi-automatic and torch from my backpack?"

He waited for the items, then, "Guard these two and shoot them if they so much as twitch," he instructed.

Sarah nodded, passed Jason the torch and stepped into place.

He lowered the shotgun, removed the live shell from the chamber, then propped the weapon up in the corner of the hall by the kitchen, dug for his key and opened the door. Jason lit the torch then quickly descended the stairs leading into the basement.

He was relieved to find the machine exactly where he had left it. He crossed to the screen and touched it to activate the display. An icon in the top right corner indicated the power was nearly out. It was into the red and he doubted there was enough left to send anyone anywhere in time, never mind so far back. He returned to the bottom of the stairs. "Is everything all right up there?" he called.

"Yes, fine."

He went back to the machine and popped open a side panel.

At first, Jason struggled to find the circuit he required; the torch light was limited and the internal connections crowded, until he sat, looking directly into the device. From there he quickly identified the chip and removed it. He wrapped it in a handkerchief to keep it safe, then put it into a zipped pocket inside his rucksack before returning upstairs and locking the door behind him.

He waved the key at the pair. "I'm taking this with me. What's in the basement is of no use to you and it would be a waste of energy breaking the door down. Now we're heading out the way that we came. Do not attempt to follow us or we will kill you," he warned.

Jason and Sarah backed away. They reached the kitchen and had just lost sight of the couple when the sound of an engine was heard in the street at the front of the house.

"That's the army," the young woman said. "They'll help us." She turned, ran along the passage and flung open the door. "You'll get your comeuppance," she called.

Jason and Sarah sprinted through the kitchen, out the door, to the back fence and into the property opposite. The layout of this garden was similar to Jason's, where a path along the side of the house allowed them access to a neighbouring road.

"That was familiar," Sarah panted.

"What?" he said, frantically looking around to check they were not being followed.

"The last time I was here with you we also ended up running through the gardens to get away from soldiers."

"I take it we made it."

"Yes, but only just. Andrews got a hold of me and threatened to cut my throat."

Jason looked at her, shocked.

She nudged her head at the scientist and smiled. "But, you saved me."

"Glad I could help," Jason said softly.

"He beat me up in Alnwick library's basement. They caught me when you were looking for information and were convinced I was stealing. Andrews was interrogating me as he could sense I was hiding something. What he didn't know was, the something was you."

They looked behind when raised voices were heard in the distance.

"Come on," Jason urged, "we'd better get going."

Chapter Twenty

Central Library, Alnwick, Northumberland

Briggs instructed he was not to be disturbed, moved to the library upstairs with Andrews and sat beside the officer, reading through the report. There was no-one else in the room; exactly how he wanted it.

Andrews shook his head as they neared the end of the booklet, his face screwed up like he had tasted something horrid. "It must be a joke."

Briggs ignored him, turned another page and continued to read.

"Time travel is not possible," Andrews stated firmly. He crossed his arms and sat back, waiting for Briggs to finish.

A further five minutes passed in silence whilst the mercenary read through every page of the report before he finally closed the booklet, inhaled deeply and pushed it across the table.

Andrews sat forward, leaning around to look at his commander. "Well, are you convinced about the possibilities of time travel or do you think this is some sort of elaborate hoax?"

Briggs' mouth tightened. He looked at the officer. "Why would anyone do such a thing in the present climate? I could understand if there hadn't been a nuclear war, but people are fighting for their lives at the moment." He stood and began to pace. "Nobody has the time or energy to go to such lengths." He stopped and waved a hand in the direction of the forest. "I mean, where the hell did he come from?"

"So what do you wanna do?"

Briggs returned to the table and picked up the report. "The scientist, Jason, said the machine was in Ponteland." He thought a moment. "Ponteland is a big place, especially if you have to search every house."

"But there's no hurry," Andrews said nonchalantly. "Things have obviously altered."

Briggs' brows furrowed. "How?"

"He said he was passed by the civilians on the road, just outside of Morpeth, as he returned to Ponteland. It's a, what..?" Andrews threw his head back, his mouth turned down as he thought a moment. He returned his attention to Briggs. "Three hours', four at the most, walk to Ponteland from there. Everything else happened in the early hours of the morning. We've been fighting here with the rebels for the past twenty-four hours or more. If the change was going to happen, it would have happened before now. Something else has altered in the meantime."

"Yes." Briggs flung his hand towards the forest again. "Him! But that doesn't mean it's going to stay changed. It could just mean he's delayed it. The only way to be sure is to either find that machine in Ponteland..."

Andrews pointed at the report. "He said it was low on charge."

Briggs nodded. "Or go find out how that fucker got here." He pulled a key from his pocket and studied the fob. "I suspect we'll find the answer in Kenton Bank Foot."

"The Territorial Army base in Kenton has a nuclear bunker beneath it."

Briggs lifted his head. "Ahh...! It's all beginning to make sense. I think we definitely need to pay a visit there."

"What about the rebels?" Andrews asked as Briggs started from the room. "They were to be killed in the morning in the town square in front of their families."

The mercenary stopped and threw his hands up, exasperated. "Damn! I forgot about them." He paused, thought a moment, then continued to the door. "Come on, we'll sort it now." He led the way from the library. "There's no time for goodbyes. Instead, we'll make an example of their bodies."

Andrews followed Briggs to a weapons store.

Briggs opened the door, retrieved two semi-automatics and some extra clips. He handed one to the sergeant, loaded the gun, removed the safety and headed to the stairs.

There were two guards watching five men tied to chairs in the basement.

"You have no right to hold us here!" one of the men yelled the moment he spotted Briggs.

Andrews immediately recognised him as one of the three men who had been sent on the mission to retrieve food from the bunker beneath the Town Moor on the northern edge of Newcastle.

The sergeant had warned them to get in and out as fast as possible as the radiation levels, although not deadly at this stage due to the rapid half-life deterioration of such high levels of emissions, would still prove fatal if they were excessively exposed. He figured specific instructions on how to enter the bunker would be enough to get them away from danger as fast as possible, but did not count on the diesel engine in the otherwise silent streets alerting another group of renegades who had also been waiting for the rads to fall enough to enter the stores.

Andrews had not been so naive as to give any of the men guns, but he figured when they entered the bunker they obviously found more than just stocks of food, water, dried fruits and grains amassed in the massive underground shelter.

The three had planned to return with more than just weapons, but the renegades arrived just as they were starting to pack the food.

Supplies were dwindling in all areas and neither party was willing to share. The gunfight that ensued led to the serious injury of one of the men, who died soon after he returned to Alnwick.

Their arrival back in the ancient town was literally explosive, when a rocket was launched at the library, which was being used as a temporary headquarters by Briggs and his men. It was a day and a half before the troops took control of the town again, after that initial failed attack, at the cost of a number of lives, not all of which were just civilians.

Andrews stepped up to the man and swiped the flat of his hand across his face.

His head cracked off to one side, the sound of the slap as painful as the impact. He looked back at the officer, his face a grim determined mask, a red, hand-shaped welt already beginning to form.

"We warned you that your families would be the first to starve if you didn't come back with the food," Andrews snarled. "You haven't got a clue what you're doing." He waved a hand at Briggs and the soldiers standing behind. "We're keeping people alive."

The man laughed. A short sharp, contemptuous laugh. "Keeping people alive! Don't flatter yourself. You're just a bunch of butchers. Captain Harrison was keeping people alive. You two," he looked at Briggs, "are just a couple of vultures. You've got people doing your dirty work because there's no protective suits, then if they don't work fast enough, hard enough, to a certain standard, their food and water is withheld, or worse, they're killed."

Andrews leaned forward until he was eye to eye with the man. "It's called martial law," he said. He stood. "If the bodies aren't buried, there'll be disease, you do as you're told, and yes, there have been some casualties, but there would have been a lot more if you'd been left to your own devices."

"Captain Harrison was protecting us," the man spat. "He was looking after the town and had the best interests of the people in everything he did."

"Enough!" Briggs barked. He stepped around, pushing Andrews back, out of the way.

For a moment a look of horror crossed the men's faces as the threat dawned, then the mercenary opened up with the gun, with carefully controlled shots. Duh, duh, duh, duh, duh! For a few seconds the noise was deafening in the enclosed basement whilst the men, still tied to their chairs, jumped with the force of the single bullets pumped into their hearts with the precision of a surgeon. Finished, Briggs spun on the soldiers standing behind. "Take their bodies to the town square and hand them over to their families. Remember to warn them if anything like this ever happens again, I'll not just kill the perpetrators, but two other family members as well."

"Yes, sir!"

Briggs strode to the stairs with Andrews immediately behind.

As they stepped out of the building an army vehicle was pulling into the car park.

The officers hurried to a jeep as the soldier emerged and called out to catch their attention.

"Sir! Captain Briggs!"

Briggs stopped.

"Sir," he panted up, "I picked up a couple of civilians in Ponteland who claimed they were assaulted by a man and a woman who wanted something in the basement of a house they were living in. The woman said that the man beat her husband up and she was threatened with a knife. I tried to find the couple, but they disappeared through the gardens. Is it all right for me to process the two that were assaulted and to give them some food?" He stepped closer and lowered his voice. "They seem to be struggling. I don't think they've had anything decent to eat in a while. They were unaware that we had set up a survival unit in Alnwick."

Briggs smiled. "Yes, that would be fine, but first, I'd like to have a quick word with them. I need to know precisely where in Ponteland they encountered this couple."

Chapter Twenty-One

En-route to Kenton Bank Foot

Jason glanced around at Sarah. “How are you doing?” He had noticed her pace had begun to slow as they once again passed the airport.

“I’m OK.” She looked up and forced a smile. “It’s amazing how deeply you sleep when you’re so exhausted you can hardly think. Twenty minutes resting in the car between the bunker and Morpeth did me the world of good. In fact,” she smiled again, but this time it was more genuine, “I’m sure it’ll keep me going for another couple of days at least.”

Jason laughed. “We could stop for a few minutes if you want.”

“No, it’s just the hill, I’m fine,” she insisted. “Once again running on adrenaline.” She looked back. “We can’t risk that soldier catching up with us. We have to keep moving.”

They continued walking for a few minutes in silence before Jason approached a difficult subject. “You do know there’s a risk you don’t exist in my timeline,” he said cautiously.

“I know, you explained,” she replied flatly.

Jason shook his head. “I can’t get used to the fact that you’ve done all this before.”

“It was slightly different the last time, but no less traumatic.”

“What happened when you went back?”

“There was only three minutes of power stored in the machine so you sent me to the town centre. There was a demonstration going on.”

“Yes, I passed through that as well.”

“There was very little time to assess the situation. I frantically searched for you, then I was bumped from behind and looked around and realised it was you. I tried to grab you, but was too late. Suddenly, I was surrounded by people as the crowd closed in and was trying to push through when I was grabbed from behind. I looked around and was horrified to see it was Briggs.”

Jason sighed. “There are now three overlaps in that time period. It’s getting pretty messy.”

“What do you mean by overlaps?”

“There is the original time period, where Hitler and his men attended a rally at Havelberg. Its first overlay was when I got involved. I appeared, accidentally killed him and stopped the Second World War happening, which led to,” he looked around solemnly, “this. The second overlay is the time period when you appeared to try to stop me killing Hitler and the third is the time period with Briggs. No matter what, we are all a permanent part of the 1930s Havelberg rally.”

“Even if I didn’t exist in the other timeline, I’d rather be dead than continue to live like this.”

“Life will recover.”

“Are you sure?” Sarah choked. “I go through the motions of life, but without my loved ones I feel dead inside.”

Jason turned his face away. “I know what you mean. The moment I entered Ponteland I found myself looking for Jessica.”

“Who’s Jessica?”

He looked back. “My wife. I never mentioned her to you?”

"No. When you came into the Town Hall and we met for the first time, I realised there was still some nice people left alive. We talked, you fed me my first decent meal in weeks and I fell asleep. I'd been having trouble sleeping because I was frightened of being discovered, but the food, the fire and you being there made me feel so safe, I went into such a deep sleep that I was barely aware of anything. At some point in the night I did hear crying. Now looking back I realise it was you because you'd discovered what you'd done. I vaguely heard you gasp 'Jessica' in amongst the sobs before I fell asleep again and I figured she was either your wife, because I did notice you were wearing a wedding ring, or maybe she could have possibly been a daughter."

The pair went silent again as they neared the precipice of the hill. At the top, Sarah stopped, turned and looked back at the road just travelled.

"That view is spectacular," she said as she stood admiring the peaks and dips of the Cheviot Hills straddling the horizon. "It's been spoiled, though, because I know that monster is up there." She turned her back to the scene and continued along the road leading to the flyover which crossed the Western Bypass over the A1.

"Is the Briggs in this timeline worse than the Briggs from my timeline?" Jason asked as the road levelled out.

"Much!" Sarah said emphatically. "He killed his own men for trying to help the weak and vulnerable. You had to work for food and if you couldn't work, you got none. The soldiers that were supposed to kill us said that a young Private was killed by Briggs because he was caught sneaking food out to the old people in Alnwick. I think that was why they rebelled, they had certainly had enough, and decided to let us go. If you ever met him, you would know what I mean. He gives you the chills."

Jason looked confused. "Surely *he* wouldn't want to live like this." He shook his head. "Nobody could want to live like this."

“It’s all about power. Why else would the Briggs from your timeline want to make sure the altered timeline was preserved? He’d rather rule in this world than be a nobody in his own.” Suddenly, she stopped, her face aghast, when she got her first glimpse of the flyover. “Oh, God!”

“This is nothing,” Jason stated. “Wait ’til you see the road underneath.”

They stepped up to the blockade of cars parked bumper to bumper, with barely enough of a gap between each vehicle to pass through.

Sarah looked right and saw the slip road leading from the motorway was clear. Instead the blockage was caused by traffic travelling away from Kenton and the areas closer to the city, to the roundabout from the west.

“They must have all been trying to head north,” she gasped.

“It’s the logical route for those from this region to follow,” Jason said as he led the way onto the roundabout and began making his way between the cars. “That, or possibly Cumbria. You have fewer cities therefore less chance of encountering bombed out areas, which equals less fallout. You also have wild deer which could be hunted for food and you’re never very far from the coast, so you could catch fish and shellfish if you’re no good at shooting.” He stopped talking long enough to shuffle across the bonnet of a car, when there was no apparent route to get around it. “Then there’s foraging and the land to grow crops. It’s understandable that people would head for hills.”

Sarah followed Jason's moves until they drew close to the barrier protecting the traffic from the twenty metre drop onto the road below. There she stopped and peered over the edge at the rows of cars, four abreast, all heading north, completely blocking both carriageways. She scanned the embankment where bodies, their decomposition slowed in the cold weather, were sprawled on the grass. Blood, darkened with decay, soaked through clothing and in most cases established the cause of death being a bullet to the chest, a shotgun to the neck or a severed artery. She returned her attention to the road and followed the line of traffic until just short of the horizon her eyes stopped on a mass of blackened fused metal.

She could not identify how many vehicles were involved as metal was twisted into metal and one car merged into another in the inferno that had ensued, with the only thing remotely recognisable being the turret of a tank protruding above the carnage.

She looked behind and could not comprehend, at first, what she was seeing until she identified the rolling blackened hills in the distance.

The scorched mounds on the far side of the Tyne had been home to over two hundred thousand people until the bomb hit the city of Newcastle and the Gateshead hills took the full force of the shockwave heading south when they helped to contain the blast.

Jason stepped up and took her by the hand.

She was looking faint, her eyes wide, her mouth open in horror.

"Come on. It's best not to look," he said softly. "We're going to stop this thing ever happening in the first place." He turned her away from the scene and continued through the cars until they cleared the jam on the opposite side of the roundabout.

Chapter Twenty-Two

En-route to Ponteland

"What are you going to do when you find them?" Andrews called over the roar of the engine. He was regretting not getting into the driver's seat fast enough, before the mercenary did.

Briggs had no fear, at least none that Andrews was aware of, and would see nothing wrong with tearing down the motorway at a hundred and fifteen miles an hour simply because there was no other traffic in the way.

Andrews, on the other hand, had seen tyres overheat and blow at high speeds, bumps in the road or even stones change the course of the wheels and send a vehicle careering off into a ditch. Since the war, though, the greatest risk on the roads came from straying animals.

The local wildlife, which now included previously domesticated horses and cattle who had escaped their enclosures, had come to see the road as any other part of the landscape now there was not a constant stream of traffic ploughing the tarmac.

Briggs had spent almost all of his time in Alnwick since his arrival six weeks ago. There was a brief period when he was away checking on the safety of a loved one, during which time Captain Harrison was killed in a raid whilst distributing food, before he returned and took charge as the highest-ranking officer. Since then, it had always been Andrews and his men that had gone outside of the ancient town to search for survivors and to organise burial parties. As a result, Briggs did not have much experience of how things had changed beyond Alnwick's borders so, a deer, horse or cow, which would cave the front of the jeep in with ease even if they were hit at half the speed they were doing, straying onto the road would not even cross his mind.

Andrews pointed at the speedo. "You might want to slow down," he called.

Briggs scowled and glanced at the officer. “What?” he snapped.

Andrews shook his head. “Never mind.” He soon realised you only made suggestions to Briggs, you never told him what to do, especially if you wanted to stay alive. He was aware his position was stronger than just about everybody in the platoon as he was definitely trusted, and trust did not come lightly to the mercenary, but still he knew there were limits, and Briggs’ limits were a lot shorter than most.

“He’s done the job and I want it to stay done. I’m going to kill them so they can’t interfere any more. Any other changes might not be congruous with our way of life.”

“Do you really want to preserve this timeline?” Andrews asked. “In five years’ time we’ll all be dead from cancer in any case.”

“You think too small,” Briggs stated. “This is just the beginning.”

“Oh!” Andrews’ attention engaged.

“We’re just getting established in Alnwick. The first crops will be planted in the next few weeks and the harvest in the autumn will allow us to take in more people. Alnwick now has the only major hospital in the region which is capable of treating a large variety of diseases and in particular cancer. Greater stocks of food will allow us to expand our farming as Northumberland is over five thousand square kilometres, a good portion of which is suitable for the growth of crops. Remember, the Romans used Corbridge as their main grain house.” He glanced smugly at the sergeant. “We’ll be like the Romans, except with heavy artillery.”

Andrews threw his head back and laughed. He remembered why he liked Briggs so much.

They travelled without speaking for a few more miles.

Briefly, a fox, then later two deer, alarmed by the sound of the engine, were glimpsed scuttling from the road before disappearing into the surrounding trees.

Andrews broke the silence. “How long do you think all of this will last?”

“What do you mean?” Briggs asked, confused.

“The road systems, the buildings,” he shrugged his shoulders, his bottom lip protruding, “you know,” he did quotation signs with his fingers, “civilisation.”

“It won’t take long for the roads to go. A few cracks and one or two bad winters later, water gets in, freezes, expands and turns them into chasms. The buildings will take a little longer, but still it’s amazing how fast the trees can reclaim. Without careful management, roots and grasses soon tear up the paths and before you know it, you have crumbling houses in the middle of a forest. Fifty years from now you’ll not recognise this place. In fact some things need constant care like the roads under rivers and I’m willing to bet, if it survived, the Tyne Tunnel is already inaccessible due to flooding.”

Andrews pointed as they passed a sign. “You might want to turn off here,” he warned, “the road up ahead is blocked.”

Briggs indicated, purely out of habit, and pulled off the motorway a short while later. His pace on the B roads was no less alarming, in fact more so due to the narrow, uneven nature of the thoroughfare and ten minutes later, when they pulled into Ponteland, Andrews breathed a silent sigh of relief.

Briggs continued with his breakneck pace through the main high street, but at least by then it was light enough to see for some distance ahead. He turned down a road running alongside a cluster of shops and continued for a further two hundred yards before turning into Willowburn Avenue and finally pulling to an abrupt halt outside of a house numbered sixty-three.

The front door stood wide open. The morning light bled into the passage enough to illuminate the bottom few steps of the stairs leading to the upper floor. Beyond the hall, the kitchen could be seen flooded in rays, but the central part of the vestibule remained gloomy and foreboding.

Briggs leapt from the car, strode up the path and entered the property with Andrews close behind.

He soon found the door leading to the basement and tried the handle. He rattled it a few times, unconvinced at first it was locked, before he instructed, "Wait here." He went back to the jeep and returned to the hallway carrying a crowbar.

The wood squealed and groaned before suddenly there was a loud crack and the door to the basement shot open.

The mercenary retrieved a small torch from a loop on his belt and swiftly descended the stairs.

Andrews stepped beyond the door, but no further; waiting at the top of the steps, he made sure they could not be accidentally locked into the basement. He slipped into darkness, the limited light from the hall unable to lift the illumination much above a shadowy grey, and watched Briggs, his face ghastly in the bleed from the beam, come to a halt at the time machine.

"It was worth the journey because at least we now know what we're looking for," Briggs called. He lowered the torch and illuminated the discarded panel. "He's definitely been here." He crouched and looked inside to examine the internal circuitry. "He appears to have taken something from one of the boards. There's an empty connection which looks out of place." He stood, slipped his hand into his pocket and removed the chip retrieved from the shooter's body. He squatted again, reached into the panels, wires and microcircuitry and popped the chip into the empty slot. Quickly, he removed it, stood, returned it to his pocket and hurried up the stairs. "Get to the car and get it started," he called. "We have to be quick. There must be another machine." He reached the hall as Andrews fired up the engine. "He's got the missing part; we have to stop him," Briggs said as he leapt into the jeep. He slipped on his belt as Andrews pulled away. "How fast can we get to Kenton?" he yelled.

Andrews remained silent as he flung the vehicle right. He did a rapid U turn, floored the accelerator and then sped for the main road. "We can reach the motorway in about fifteen minutes, but we might have to walk from there."

Briggs nodded. "OK, make sure it's a little faster."

Chapter Twenty-Three

En-route to Kenton Bank Foot

Andrews glanced at the mercenary. "It's really exciting."

"What is?"

"A time machine. You could go anywhere and do anything."

"Yeah!" Briggs snorted. "If you wanted to decimate time and come back to God knows what!" He looked at the sergeant pointedly. "You've seen what he's done. There's been a nuclear war where there shouldn't have been one and all because he tried to go back and help his grandmother with a little bit of money."

Andrews smiled. "You've got to admire how clever he is though."

"I admire nothing!" Briggs snapped. "He was an idiot using it in the first place. Then taking a gun...!" He screwed his face up in disgust. "You don't use a gun unless you know what you're doing."

Andrews waved a hand at the windscreen when they caught sight of the blockade. "There you go. See what I mean."

A few minutes later he pulled the jeep to a halt and the pair climbed out onto the road.

"OK," Briggs snapped, full of business, "let's kit up and get moving." He stepped around to the back of the vehicle and opened the boot. He passed Andrews a single shot handgun and a semi-automatic.

The sergeant shoved both into a holster slung around his waist, grabbed a couple of extra clips and secured them into a pocket at the back of his trousers. He stepped around from the jeep and moved up to the cars on the roundabout blocking their path. He was tracing a route with his eyes through the barrier when suddenly movement up ahead distracted his attention. He looked at the source and saw two figures nearing the top of the hill on the opposite side of the blockade. Quickly, he returned to his commander.

Briggs had loaded his weapon and was about to lock the car when the sergeant came panting up. "What's wrong?" he asked.

"There are two people running up the hill leading to Kenton Bank Foot." Andrews rummaged briefly in the back of the jeep before emerging with a pair of binoculars. He moved clear of the vehicle and examined the couple more closely.

"Well?" Briggs prompted.

"It's definitely a man and a woman. She looks like she pretty much belongs here, well wrapped up and rather unkempt, but he looks out of place. He has a rucksack, but he's wearing a long wool overcoat, the sort that you'd wear with a suit."

"Right!" Briggs snapped. "We can do it here." He returned to the boot, loaded a rifle and came back to the front to use the bonnet as a prop to steady the weapon. "Which one should I kill first?" he sneered.

"The guy. She probably doesn't even know how to use the machine."

"OK, good idea." Briggs kneeled, propped his elbows on the bonnet, steadied the gun and squinted through the sights. Moments later he had his crosshairs firmly fixed on Jason's head. Then he gently squeezed the trigger.

Chapter Twenty-Four

En-route to Kenton Bank Foot

The morning mist, visible at first dawn, had started to lift, but had left behind a slick coating on the sooty residue covering the road.

There was some debris towards the bottom of the hill. Tiles and chimneys, blasted off rooftops, and branches torn from the surrounding trees sparsely littered the road, but the nearer to the top the pair drew, the more cluttered the way became due to the numerous properties and their proximity to the bomb.

Sarah stopped. "What's that?"

Jason carried on a few paces further before turning back to look at her. "What? I can't hear anything."

"Shush!" she hissed.

The pair stood silent, straining to listen for a sound that she was not entirely sure existed. Then suddenly, "There. Do you hear it?" she whispered.

Jason opened his mouth to protest again that he could hear nothing when suddenly he picked up the faint sound of an engine some way off in the distance. He looked at Sarah with a growing sense of doom. "It's either a jeep or a lorry."

"Yes, I agree. There's definitely a diesel engine involved."

"Come on," Jason urged. "We need to get going." He took Sarah's hand and they began to run up the hill as fast as the road conditions and debris allowed.

Shattered bricks, plasterboard, blankets, toys, clothing all cluttered their way as they pushed towards the pinnacle, where they could reach the bunker a hundred yards from there.

The hum of the engine drew louder, the exact location difficult to identify as the noise, unhindered by any other sounds, bounced off the natural dips and peaks of the surrounding landscape. There was a screech as the vehicle came to a halt, then all other noises, apart from the gasps of the pair desperately trying to get up the hill as fast as possible, stopped.

Jason pulled on Sarah's arm as she struggled more and more to keep up. The higher they climbed the greater her reliance on him to pull her along. Then suddenly he slipped, skidding on a piece of fallen timber, and they both hit the ground.

As he landed on the rubble, chest first, he heard a loud crack and immediately thought it was a piece of wood snapping beneath the bricks, until there was another. This time it was closer and when a tile just right of his head shattered, it dawned on him what it was. "We're being shot at!" he screamed. "Get behind the walls and stay low."

They scrambled to their feet and, staying stooped, hurried to a cluster of partially demolished houses near the road.

A number of shots came in quick succession with at least one frighteningly close when a piece of shrapnel tore through Jason's coat.

The scientist, too hyped and too scared to even notice, pressed on towards the ruined buildings until he passed behind the relative safety of a shattered wall, dragging Sarah behind him.

Gasping for air, her chest heaving visibly through the layers of clothing, Sarah raised herself up, looking away from the shooting, towards their destination. "I can see the bunker from here," she blurted.

"That's all very well," Jason panted, "but we have to get there alive." He looked around for a way through the rubble, before pointing to a tunnel shaped by a partially collapsed wall. "Come on, that should help to keep us safe."

Gingerly, they picked their way over the debris, which moved and tumbled with every step.

"I can see the road," Jason said, elated, as they passed beyond the houses, "and there's a way through."

Sarah glanced back as they cleared the rubble and started towards the mound, which housed the entrance to the bunker.

Two men were running up the hill at a fast pace, closing the gap between the couple, too swiftly for comfort.

"We're not going to make it!" she screamed. "Leave me behind. Go alone."

Jason's thoughts paused a moment as he reluctantly looked at what he knew he must do. He slowed, stared at the men coming rapidly up the hill behind them, locked wide eyes with Sarah's, then released her hand and began to pull away.

Sarah lowered her head and pushed on. Her mind focused on the bunker. She had to make it or die trying. She was struggling with a number of things – running, breathing – but her mounting panic gave her an advantage when a much needed boost found her pace staying relative with Jason's. She glanced up as she crossed the road.

He was at the top of the mound, then moments later he disappeared into the pipe leading to the bunker.

Her breathing was coming in short sharp desperate gasps as she reached the bank and started up, her pace slowing considerably once she hit the slope.

The sound of machine gunfire caused her to stoop and a rapid change of direction, which took her off the shortest route into the tunnel, led to cover from shrubbery and debris.

She risked a glance back when a gap in the bushes allowed a view of the road and saw the two men had reached the top of the hill and had turned towards the Territorial Army base.

She returned her attention forward, her muscles screaming, her lungs heaving, and spotted the entrance to the pipe up ahead. She pumped her arms, using everything in her arsenal, to push herself on, then just short of the entrance she saw Jason emerging from the bunker.

"Get inside!" he screamed as he ran past her in the opposite direction.

Sarah kept going and arrived at the door in a near state of collapse. She lurched and wobbled and with the last of her strength, pulled open the barrier before falling through the door onto the concrete floor beyond. She pushed herself up onto her knees, then dragged herself to her feet using a rail around the wall. There she waited for vital seconds, steadying herself before starting down the ladder, holding the rungs tightly for fear she would fall.

Jason turned right and continued up the mound, which was used to disguise the bunker in peace time and protect it from the blast. Quickly, he ascended to the top, using his hands for extra leverage, and looked around the vicinity.

Her breathing slowed and the walls stopped swimming as Sarah descended the ladder, and by the time she reached the bottom, her heart rate had decreased to a more reasonable level.

She turned and grabbed the door to pass into the main part of the bunker, then froze when she heard a string of explosions coming from outside.

Chapter Twenty-Five

Territorial Army Base, Kenton Bank Foot

"Spread out," Briggs ordered. He pointed for Andrews to go left and follow Sarah's longer route around the bushes whilst he took the shorter, but more obstacle-littered path, up the bank.

The sergeant moved around, using the bushes for cover until he caught sight of the entrance to the bunker. He studied the pipe for a few seconds to confirm it was empty before making his way closer, using the shrubbery for cover, until he had a good view of the door at the far end. Once there he looked around for Briggs and soon spotted the mercenary halfway up the bank.

He scanned the vicinity and found no sign of the couple and presumed they must have moved inside. He started forward, cautiously at first, but as he saw Briggs nearing the top of the embankment, broke free and ran towards the pipe.

From the top of the hill, Jason spotted one of the men dashing for the bunker. He looked around, but still could not see the other. Quickly, he stooped and drew the pins from each of the four grenades at his feet. He checked his watch. They all had a fifteen-second timer, so he did not want to throw them too soon. Five seconds passed before he started to lob them in a semi-circular motion, with the last landing a few paces ahead of the man running to the shelter.

For a split second Andrews thought the device was a small ball, belonging to either a child or a dog – there were a lot of personal belongings amongst the wreckage – until he spotted the trigger. Already he knew stopping in time was no longer an option. Instead he picked up the pace and leapt over the grenade, putting as much distance between himself and the bomb as possible. He landed safely and flung himself towards the ground just as the first of the four exploded.

Each of the grenades had a fifteen-metre burst, which expanded up and out from the device. On the ground Andrews would have been protected from the cone-shaped spread of shrapnel, but he could not get down fast enough to get below the level of the second blast. Instead, several pieces of the grenade's metal casing and internal ball bearings, inserted to make the device more deadly, tore into the sergeant's shoulders, neck and head, killing him before he hit the ground.

Jason paused just long enough to check that Andrews was not getting up before he hurried back down the hill, taking the steepest descent for speed, and ran into the tunnel leading to the bunker.

Instinctively, Briggs dived for cover the moment he heard the low clunk of metal hitting the soil in various locations above his head. He hurled himself backwards down the bank and scrambled off to one side, then flung himself over a small wall for protection, just as the first of the grenades exploded. Three more blasts followed in close succession, with the final one spraying hot debris over the mercenary when the device detonated on top of a brick, wedged into the soil, close by.

Briggs waited a few seconds to check there would be no more explosions before leaping out from behind the wall and running up the embankment as fast as he could, his gun at the ready.

He scanned the vicinity as he reached the edge of the shrubbery and immediately spotted Andrews' body lying unmoving and bloodied several metres away. He ignored the cadaver and checked to see if the woman and scientist were outside before breaking cover and quickly making his way into the tunnel.

Chapter Twenty-Six

Territorial Army Base, Kenton Bank Foot

Sarah was standing at the bottom of the ladder, shining the torch up to illuminate the rungs, anxiously waiting for Jason to appear.

The outside door went and she shrunk away from the base, lowered the light and had just extinguished the beam when she recognised the footfalls.

Her fear of the military, brought on by Briggs, had produced one advantage in that she could now identify the sound of an army boot on concrete, as opposed to any other type of shoe.

She switched on the torch and returned to her position at the bottom of the ladder. "What happened?" she called when Jason looked over the brink.

"I threw four grenades to make them think twice about approaching the tunnel. It might have only slowed one of them down, but I think the other one might be dead. If he's not, he's very badly injured." He reached the bottom of the ladder and turned to face Sarah. "He hit the ground, then never moved and there was a lot of blood."

Sarah pushed the door open and stepped into the corridor beyond the stairwell. "Grenades? Where did you find them?"

"When I was waiting for you to return from Morpeth, I had plenty of time to look around. There's a weapons store, just to the right of the kitchen, in the living quarters."

She held the door open for Jason to pass through. "Did you get a good look at the men?" She released the barrier and allowed it to close.

"I got a good look at the one I think might be dead."

"What did he look like?" Sarah asked cautiously.

"He was quite tall, slim and had very light brown, almost blonde hair."

Her face furrowed. “That sounds like Andrews, Briggs’ second-in-command.”

Jason paused at the door.

“Do you think...?”

The scientist was not listening. He turned the switch just below the handle several times then, “I can’t lock the door!” he exclaimed, panicked.

Sarah looked at him, shocked. “What? Has he smashed it?”

“Yes!” Jason screamed.

She pulled on his sleeve. “Come on. We have to go. If that was Andrews, then there’s a good chance the other man is Briggs.” She lit the way down the corridor to the room at the far end. “I caught a glimpse of them as they ran up the hill and one of the men certainly looked like he could have passed for Briggs.”

Inside the room Jason moved to the table, dragged it across the floor and shoved it in front of the door. “I’m sure it won’t do much, but it might buy us a few seconds.” He stopped a moment to speak to Sarah. “The big question is, which Briggs are we talking about here; the Briggs from this timeline or the Briggs from my timeline?”

Sarah shrugged. “Well, if Andrews is with him, then it must be the Briggs from this timeline.”

Jason moved to the machine and pointed to the panel. “Shine the torch there,” he instructed. He waited for her to comply before he slipped off the cover, removed the chips from the secured pocket inside his rucksack and popped them into their empty slots on the circuit board inside the unit. He stood. “Not necessarily. You reckon they were identical, so the Briggs from my timeline may have planned to replace the Briggs in this timeline all along.”

“Either way,” Sarah said, exasperated, “we do not want to mess with them, whichever timeline they’re from.”

Jason nodded. “True.” He turned to the unit, “Here goes,” switched on the machine and touched the screen to activate the device.

Lights danced across the display, then a string of commands ran down the screen for a few seconds, before a menu appeared and waited for further instructions.

He checked the level of the battery, then threw back his head. “Thank you!” he screamed when it showed nearly full. He looked at Sarah and beamed. “Right!” He turned his attention to the screen. “I’ll pull up my original journey.” He tapped the display several times, dragged his finger down a scrollbar and touched an entry towards the bottom. “I’ll adjust the power so we’re not stuck for several hours and move the location slightly so we don’t arrive at my grandmother’s house. And... done!” He took Sarah’s arm. “Get into the machine.”

She shook her head. “I’m not going through again,” she squawked. “I think you should do it now we know meeting yourself doesn’t cause annihilation.”

He opened the door and bustled her in. “I wasn’t going to send you alone, we’re both going.” He touched the start button to initiate the countdown and joined Sarah inside.

“Will it be able to distinguish between you and me,” she asked breathlessly.

“To be honest I’ve never tried it,” Jason confessed, “but I’ve never materialised with my clothes merged with my skin, so there’s no reason why it shouldn’t.”

A low distant boom caused the pair to look panicked towards the door.

“He’s inside the bunker,” Jason said as a tingling sensation travelled through his muscles, all the way down to his bones, then the room disappeared.

Chapter Twenty-Seven

Territorial Army Base, Kenton Bank Foot

Briggs ran to the bunker, without so much as a glance to see if his second-in-command was still alive or not. He opened the door, then paused, when he saw the edge of the chute slipping into blackness, to pull a torch from his belt. He stepped inside, a foot still wedging the barrier open, and cautiously leaned forward to shine the beam into the chamber.

It barely illuminated the floor twenty metres down, but it was enough to see there was no-one waiting in ambush at the base. The barrier boomed shut behind him, echoing in the chute, as he moved onto the ladder and hurried down the rungs.

A minute later, he arrived at the bottom, readied his gun and checked the corridor before stepping out into the passage and cautiously looking around.

He knew how these places worked, several rooms running off a central spine with further connecting chambers could make a bunker as complex and extensive as a rabbit warren. Searching for someone could be laborious and potentially dangerous with numerous ambush points and plenty of places to find yourself trapped.

He moved deeper into the passage and had just approached the first door when a strange whining noise came from the room at the far end. He changed direction and decided to check that one out first.

At the bottom of the corridor, Briggs stopped and pushed against the door to gently open it. He was surprised to encounter resistance. He could see it was not locked, but there was something in the way, blocking the opening. He put his shoulder against the metal and pushed hard to force his way in. A scraping, squealing noise could be heard from the other side of the door. He slipped into the room when the opening was wide enough and saw the cause was a table deliberately set to obstruct the entrance.

The whining noise had stopped, but Briggs immediately saw the machine was active. He moved to the control panel and realised it was going through a cycle.

"Just over a minute," he laughed, "you're just over a minute ahead of me." He opened his jacket and slipped the booklet out from an inside pocket. "Don't get too cocky, a minute's not very long, I'll not be far behind you."

Quickly, he read the instructions, checked the previous entry, duplicated the information, then stepped into the machine and readied his gun. "You don't think you can mess with me and get away with it, do you?" he sneered, then in a blink he was gone.

Chapter Twenty-Eight

Havelberg, Germany, March 1930

The station whistle blew. Jason waved as the train began to pull away. Brushing any foreboding aside, he again reassured himself he had done the right thing.

As the last of the carriages moved away from the platform, he checked the station clock; it was 5.32 p.m. Everything had gone smoothly and he now found himself with a couple of hours to wait before returning home. He looked around. He suddenly realised how dark it had become. The station, although hardly glowing, was still well-lit, but beyond, the blackness was pitch. With the train gone, the solitude seemed emphasised. The urge to seek the comfort of street lighting and the company of others became irresistible.

It took only a few minutes at a brisk pace for Jason to find himself once again back on the main street. His feeling of comfort was short-lived, though.

Stormtroopers, backed by SS guards, were in the town square and were stopping people to ask them questions.

The last thing in the world Jason wanted was to be confronted by these Nazis. He looked around for somewhere quiet to sit for the next couple of hours and noticed a cinema across the road. He moved over and hurried inside.

The girl behind the counter informed him the film had already begun.

"Yes, that's fine." He handed over the money.

Shrugging her shoulders, she passed him a ticket.

Inside the cinema, Jason settled into a seat discreetly positioned towards the back. The film was a tragic love story; a marriage was coming apart after the death of their child.

"Excuse me, sir!"

Jason woke with a start. He looked around, alarmed.

"Excuse me, sir, the film finished ten minutes ago, you'll have to leave."

He stared at the girl blankly for a moment before suddenly remembering where he was.

"You'll have to leave now or I'll call the manager," she said, her voice sharpening with fear.

Jason shook his head. "There's no need. I'm sorry." He stood. "I'll go at once."

He hurried from the cinema, through the foyer and out the front door.

"Hello, Jason."

He stopped abruptly and turned to look at the woman.

She had been standing to one side of the door as he left. He had barely noticed her and had only caught a glimpse of her as he stepped outside. No-one should be speaking to him, as the only two that knew who he was were on the train to Hamburg, but she not only knew his name, she also spoke to him in English.

She looked distinctly unkempt and appeared to have been sleeping rough. Her auburn hair was matted in places and her face was gaunt and pale. Her clothing was dirty with mud stains on the knees, stomach and elbows as if she had been crawling across the ground. Still, despite all of this, Jason could see a strength and fire in her eyes that said a lot more about the woman than her scruffy appearance.

He gathered his thoughts. He had to be careful. He had heard about people being tricked into giving themselves away when they were questioned in English and they responded in kind.

"I do not understand you," he replied in German.

She smiled. "I know who you are." She leaned closer. "You're a time traveller and you must do exactly what I say." She nudged her head towards the cinema. "We just need somewhere to hide for a few minutes. Can we go back inside?"

Jason's face fell; he shook his head. "No, they're closing. Something went wrong," he added softly.

"There, I knew you were clever," the woman called over her shoulder. She returned her attention to Jason. "I'm Sarah and this is, well..."

Jason jumped back when the man who emerged from the shadows by the side of the building looked exactly like his twin. His face paled. "What the hell happened?"

"It's all right, you don't have to worry about us meeting," the scientist stated. "We've already proved it doesn't cause annihilation when Sarah met herself in another timeline."

"How many timelines are there?" Jason asked.

"Just the two that we know of, but this is the fourth alteration of this time zone."

Jason's eyes widened.

The scientist checked his watch. "Three minutes." He looked at Sarah. "There's a doorway under a fire escape, down this alley, which should easily accommodate us all. We can hide there until we're recalled. Come on." He led the way.

The street lighting did not reach very far down the alley and they were soon plunged into darkness, compounded by the closeness and height of the grey stone buildings lining the lane.

Carefully, the group made their way to a metal staircase. It was attached to the side of the cinema and would obviously be used to evacuate the upstairs patrons from the theatre if there was ever a fire. They moved around, beneath the steps, then slipped into the blackness of the doorway until they were sure they could not be seen from the main street.

"Why are we hiding?" Jason asked.

"You'll find out later," Sarah replied, "but for the time being I suggest we be very quiet."

The scientist checked his watch. "Two and a half minutes to go," he whispered.

****

For a moment Briggs looked around surprised, slightly disorientated by his arrival. The almost instantaneous journey from the small cubicle to the wide brightly lit street, in comparison to the blackened nuclear bunker, was a little unsettling, until he caught sight of the square and immediately gained his focus.

There were two people he was looking for: one he would recognise immediately and the other, as he did not exist in his timeline, he would have to identify by his location and his bodyguards. Both men he intended to kill and anybody else who got in his way.

There were noises up ahead that sounded like a demonstration. He moved forward and soon saw the cause of the commotion when the street opened out into the square. It was very busy with people. A protest was taking place and there was a lot of banner waving and chanting at a group of soldiers.

Briggs made his way into the crowd.

The report had stated that Hitler had been killed as he exited a building across from the square. He scanned the perimeter.

There were streets joining the plaza on his left and his right, but directly ahead was a road running parallel and across from there, a line of official-looking buildings.

He started to move through the crowd, scanning for a familiar face, and had crossed more than half of the square to a location where the mob was thinning when suddenly he saw a man grab a woman from behind. It was not so much the gesture that caught his attention, but the woman's reaction.

All around he could hear people talking, but he knew nothing of what they were saying as he spoke no German, then suddenly as if all other noises had stopped, he recognised some words coming through and in amongst them the most familiar one of them all, his name.

Tellingly, she began to pull away and Briggs saw the flash of a blade. This was all the confirmation the mercenary needed. With perfect fluidity, he raised his gun from the discreet position flung at his side and in a single movement lifted it to a right angle to his body, fired four shots at the man, moving up his chest and into the head, lowered the gun back down to conceal it by his leg and continued on his journey to the building across the square without so much as even a faltered step.

The woman screamed in fright and lifted her hands to her face as the man's body jerked three times in quick succession before finally the side of his head exploded.

Eyes wide, jaw dropped as though in alarm, fingers still wrapped around the woman's arm, the cadaver fell to the ground and landed in a crumpled heap at her feet.

She gathered her senses and looked at the shooter just before his pace took him out of sight. Briefly, she seemed totally confused and glanced at the man at her feet before her brain, hyper with terror, put all the pieces together.

She lifted her gun. It only had one shot and she had been instructed to use it in an emergency. She aimed. For a fraction of a second she had a clear target, then suddenly the crowd closed around her. She lowered the gun and pushed ahead, forcing her way through the mass until again she had a good shot. Quickly, she raised the gun, aimed and fired.

Briggs stopped when the bullet skimmed past his shoulder, tearing a hole through his jacket and grazing the skin. He turned to face the woman.

She was looking past him at the building directly opposite, where three men could be seen descending the stairs.

The two leading the way were wearing uniforms and appeared to be guards, but the man behind, dressed in a suit and a long overcoat, looked more like an official than a soldier.

The woman began to panic; she was running out of time and the time traveller was nowhere to be seen. She should have been celebrating, even though his absence was puzzling, but it was now obvious someone else was here to do the job instead. “He’s going to kill Hitler,” she screamed as the two guards stepped onto the path.

Briggs raised his gun, ready to kill her, and was just about to fire when suddenly she disappeared, wrestled to the ground by vigilantes who had witnessed her shooting the weapon.

She struggled to get free. “Stop it! Leave me alone,” she screamed, “he’s going to kill Hitler.”

****

The scientist and Sarah looked at each other, alarmed, when they heard the single gunshot ring out from the square.

He lowered his rucksack and retrieved the semi-automatic from inside the bag.

Sarah grabbed his arm, her face awash with terror. “You can’t. This is how it all started.”

“I now know what I’m doing,” he stated firmly. “I won’t make the same mistake again. Wait here,” he instructed. He moved away from the stairs and was nearing the exit from the alley when a woman screamed out a warning about Hitler in English. He picked up the pace and hurried into the street to see the crowd stampeding from the plaza. As the hordes parted, scattering for cover, he saw Briggs dead on the ground and two men holding a woman down with a couple of soldiers standing over them.

A short distance away, another man was turning from the scene and the scientist suddenly realised this was also Briggs.

“So we meet,” he muttered. “Sarah was right, you are the Briggs from her timeline.”

The mercenary continued towards the group of buildings on the far side of the square.

The scientist started sprinting, his gun at the ready. He had very little confidence in his skills as a gunman at the best of times, but at a run, he had even less. He could not risk randomly shooting as he could not afford to kill anyone else, especially the wretch they had come to save. He charged across the square. "He's going to kill Hitler," he yelled in German, just as Briggs began firing.

Neither of the guards protecting the official had time to react and were dead before they hit the ground. Then Briggs aimed at his main target and pulled the trigger as the man scrambled for cover.

The scientist fired a round, but his aim was off-centre and he caught Briggs on his left shoulder when he had been shooting at his back. It was enough to throw the mercenary's crack shot off a little, but not enough to prevent him hitting his mark.

The scientist stopped. "Nooo!" he screamed as he saw the official collapse onto the path. Suddenly, his skin started tingling. It travelled through his muscles all the way to his bones. For a fraction of a second, just before he was recalled, he saw the soldiers starting to shoot, and in a blink, he was gone.

Chapter Twenty-Nine

Kenton Bank Foot

Jason looked around wildly when he materialised in the machine with Sarah standing beside him.

"What happened?" she howled. "Why are we back here?"

He stepped out of the unit. "I saw Briggs shoot Hitler just before I was recalled."

She burst into tears, "Nooo!" and lowered her face into her hands. "I can't do this anymore. I can't live like this." She began to sob, her chest heaving, her shoulders tight.

"Come on," Jason said briskly, ignoring her breakdown. He pulled on her arm. "Get out."

She stepped out of the machine, still crying, following his instructions robotically.

He pushed her towards the door. "We're going to finish this with Briggs once and for all. I want you out of the room."

She turned to the machine, her face contorted in pain. "What? He's coming back here?" she bawled.

Jason readied his gun. "It was your Briggs that killed Hitler. You were right. It must have been him and Andrews that attacked us on the hill."

Sarah froze. "The Briggs from Alnwick?"

"Yes."

"He'll kill us for sure!" She started to drag Jason from the room. "He'll kill us both. We need to leave!"

"Not if I kill him first," Jason said. He pulled his sleeve free.

Sarah grabbed his arm, unwilling to be brushed off. "Dismantle the machine and leave him there," she pleaded.

Jason shook his head. “No. Goodness knows what damage he could do if left to his own devices. We have to get him out of that timeline and the moment he materialises, I’ll kill him. Killing him is the only way to stop him.” He pushed Sarah away. “Now get out of the room, quick.”

“No, I’m staying with you,” she said firmly.

“Then get behind me,” Jason ordered.

She jumped behind the scientist, needing no more persuading, when suddenly the whine of the machine starting up came from the device.

Jason braced himself, his heart racing, his chest thumping, gun pointing at the clear cubicle set to automatic for maximum spread, ready for the mercenary’s return. His muscles taught, his shoulders locked, he watched, unwilling to even blink, waiting for the killer to materialise.

Then suddenly he was there and Jason’s finger twitched on the trigger. Just in time, he stopped himself, as the rain of bullets would have obliterated the machine.

“What do you think happened?” Sarah whispered from behind.

Jason never spoke. He cautiously approached the unit, unconvinced it was not a ruse.

Sarah followed behind, hanging on to the back of his coat. “Is he dead?”

Jason lowered himself down to examine the bullet-riddled body more closely. “It certainly looks like it.” He stood and looked at Sarah. “Just before I disappeared the soldiers in the square started shooting at Briggs, but I presumed after I’d seen the way he killed Hitler and his guards that there was a chance he’d shoot his way out of that one as well.”

“He must have been outnumbered.”

“Yes,” Jason turned away from the body, “but how many did he kill in the process?” His shoulders slumped and his head dropped. He stood like that for a few seconds, staring at the floor before gathering himself together. “Come on.” He shuffled from the room. “I want to check Andrews is really dead,” he sighed, “then we’ll get some sleep here and make a decision about what to do with this mess when we’re rested.”

They stopped at the end of the passage.

“It’s been a while since I slept in a bed,” Sarah said. “Those couches in the Town Hall were not too bad, but you can’t stretch out the way you can in a proper bed.” She suddenly realised they were no longer moving. “What’s wrong?”

“The door’s locked. Briggs must have destroyed the lock after he returned from Germany.” Jason turned the circular handle clockwise two full rotations before the mechanism engaged and the door sprung open. He pulled it wide and stepped into the chamber. He lowered his rucksack to the ground. “You stay here, just in case there’s trouble.” He flung the gun over his shoulder and started up the ladder.

Sarah watched as Jason ascended the rungs and a couple of minutes later he disappeared from sight when he arrived at the top of the chute. She heard the outside door open then close before everything went silent, bar the whoosh of blood pounding in her ears.

When a few minutes passed and Sarah still could not hear anything, she began to regret not going with Jason as her imagination started to run wild. Maybe he had been killed; Andrews also liked to carry a knife as they discovered on their last encounter with him, or maybe he had had an accident. Another minute passed and she could stand it no longer, even gunfire would have been preferable to the torturous silence; she decided to go up the ladder. Suddenly, the outer door clattered and Sarah shrank against the side of the chute in case it was Andrews at the top of the chamber.

"Sarah!"

She returned to the bottom of the ladder when she heard Jason's voice. "What took you so long? I began to..."

"Get up here!" he called breathlessly.

She started up the rungs, the urgency in his voice commanding immediate attention. "What is it?" she yelled, but the outside door went again and Jason disappeared without a response.

Several scenarios ran through Sarah's mind and her pace faltered when she decided he may have encountered troops gathering survivors.

"Why run off," she muttered. "Talk to me first. You don't know this place. You stay away from everyone." She arrived at the top of the ladder. "We're definitely done for now." She stepped up to the door and reluctantly pushed it open.

A waft of fresh, spring air assaulted her nostrils, a background drone she had become unaccustomed to enveloped her ears and a brightness unhindered by clouds dirtied with nuclear fallout caused her to blink rapidly as her pupils struggled to adjust. She stepped outside and saw Jason standing at the end of the pipe.

He waved a hand. "Come," he said, beaming so widely it appeared as though his face had split in two. "Everything is all right."

At first Sarah thought she had misheard him, not daring to believe anything could be all right ever again. "What?" She started towards him, her fatigue fading.

"I don't know how, but everything is back to normal," Jason screamed ecstatically.

She ran towards him, her elation increasing as more of the outside world became visible.

Grass was growing beyond the edge of the pipe, a tower block came into view and the vaporous, telltale signs of air traffic streaked the sky.

She stepped outside and looked around.

The morning rush hour was in full flow and cars shuffled bumper to bumper along the road at the bottom of the bank.

Sarah fell to her knees and began to sob with relief; it was some time before she recovered enough to compose herself.

"I'm sorry I was so arrogant as to think I could interfere in time and not pay the consequences," Jason said. "Please forgive me."

She looked up, her face streaked where days of grime and dirty dust had been washed away by the salty droplets, and gently nodded. "What are you going to do?"

"Before we leave I'll dismantle the main motherboard, so no-one else can use it. I'll have to talk to General Worthing and make him understand exactly how dangerous using this machine is. I'll also have to tell him about Briggs, as no doubt someone'll find his body eventually and he may well be reported missing. I'll then have to go back to the beginning with my research into teleportation and find out where I went wrong when I introduced live matter to the system."

"Sounds good to me."

"What about you?"

Sarah smiled. "I'm going home to see my parents." She sighed, her face suddenly pained. "I haven't seen them for nearly two months and I thought I would never see them again."

Jason helped her to stand. He looked her up and down. "What, looking like that?"

She pushed a hand against her hair, then gave up when it jumped back into exactly the same position. "I never thought..." She looked uncomfortable. "You're right. I can't walk through the door looking like this."

"We'll sort out that board, then I'll get us a taxi and you can come to my place and get cleaned up. My wife is about your size, you can take some of her clothes."

Chapter Thirty

Ponteland

Jason rapped the knocker. He waited a moment, then tried again when nobody answered.

Sarah began to pace. "This is definitely your house?"

"Yes."

"By definitely, I mean... Well, you know what I mean," she said, her voice trailing off.

He shot her a nervous look, moved to the window and was just about to look inside when the front door opened.

Jessica stared at Sarah. "Can I help you?" then, "Jason," she said, surprised, when he returned to the path. Her brow furrowed. "What are you doing out here and where's your key?"

"I'll explain in a minute, we just have to get inside."

Jessica moved back to make room for the pair. "Hello," she said as Sarah stepped into the house.

Sarah smiled, uncomfortably aware of her dishevelled appearance. "Hello, I'm Sarah."

"Jessica, Jason's..."

"Wife, yes I know," Sarah said.

Jason stopped. "And sweetheart," he pointed outside, "can you pay the taxi?"

Jessica turned wide questioning eyes to her husband before she grabbed her purse and headed for the road.

Later over breakfast, Jason brought his wife up to date.

"I can't even imagine what you've been through," Jessica said to Sarah, "but to have survived that, is incredible." She looked at her empty plate, mopped clean with bread. "Have you had enough to eat?"

"Yes," Sarah said. "I can't remember the last time I felt this full. It was always just barely enough to get by and towards the end, not even that."

"We'll have to get you cleaned up," Jessica said, "so you can get back to your family."

Sarah smiled. "That would be nice."

"And clothes?" Jason reminded.

"You can have anything you want. I think we're roughly the same size, although it might be a little slack because you've lost so much weight. I'm sure we can sort something out." She led Sarah from the room and guided her upstairs.

Jason looked around the kitchen. The last time he was here he was fighting for his life, although the decor was slightly different at the time.

He stood, moved to the living room and scanned a bookcase to the left of the fireplace. He never thought he would be relieved to see a history book about World War Two sitting on the top shelf. He slipped it from its place and flicked through to a chapter dedicated to the activities of Hitler prior to him becoming chancellor, before the start of the war. Halfway down the second page the rally was mentioned in Havelberg and how an attempt on Hitler's life had resulted in a non-life-threatening injury. A woman was apprehended, but managed to get away, along with her male accomplice, who was shot several times before he escaped.

Jason closed the book. The front door opened, as he returned it to the shelf.

"Hellooo!" a familiar voice called.

He turned to face the hall, just as his mother passed the lounge.

She stopped and came back when she saw him in the room. "Where's Jessica, darling? Did she tell you we were going shopping this morning?" She continued towards the kitchen. "You'll not want to come; I know how much you hate being dragged from store to store."

Jason followed behind, fighting to control his emotions. He watched her for a while, as she made a cup of tea, relishing her company. "I would love to come shopping with you," he finally choked, "it seems like for ever since we spent any time together."

Epilogue

Sarah waved from the back of the taxi as the car pulled away. As they left the housing estate and entered the main high street running through Ponteland, she settled into the seat and revelled in its softness and comfort.

She had no idea how long it would take her body to recover and, her emotional state, she thought never would.

The closer she got to Gosforth, the more excited she became, but the greater her nerves.

She was shocked when she saw herself in the mirror after her bath and did not know how she was going to explain her appearance to her mother. Pale and gaunt, she looked almost skeletal compared to her healthy appearance.

The taxi picked up speed as they left Ponteland behind and headed towards the motorway.

The tightness in Sarah's throat increased as the gradient climbed and by the time they stopped at the roundabout, she was feeling positively sick. She looked out the window, then turned away, focusing on the back of the driver's seat when she remembered less than six hours ago she was running for her life on this very spot. She relaxed when the driver turned left rather than going straight on, which would have taken her past the bunker. She was unsure at this stage of how she would react and feared another meltdown in the back of the cab.

He picked up the pace further and before long they turned off the motorway and joined the smaller B roads which led to her street.

Sarah's heart increased and she began to feel sick again as the taxi pulled to a stop outside of the small semi-detached house. She paid the fare, got out of the cab and walked up the path to the front door. Then suddenly she realised, like Jason, she did not have a key. She tried the handle and was relieved to find it open.

She stepped into the house and was halfway down the hall when her mother came out of the kitchen, drying her hands.

She looked at Sarah, shocked.

Sarah suppressed a panic when it crossed her mind that she might not belong here.

“What are you doing home?” her mum asked. “You only went to work a few hours ago.”

Sarah paused, her mind racing for a plausible answer. “I wasn’t feeling well,” she said, hushed.

Her mum came closer and brushed her hair away from her face. She looked alarmed. “You look terrible.” She put down the towel and crossed to the phone. “I’ll call a doctor.”

“No, I’ll be fine,” Sarah said. “I’m feeling much better now.” She moved and embraced her mother. “I just needed to be with my mum.”

The End.

About the Author

I have enjoyed writing stories all my life. I also have a fascination for astronomy and science and would lie in bed from a very young age looking at the stars.

I joined a local astronomy group when I received my first telescope at Christmas a number of years ago. Since then I've enjoyed many a night, freezing until I can't stand it anymore, looking at the delights of the Universe and the magical wonders of alien worlds.

I started my career in computing, but presently work at a college helping students improve their maths and English. The rest of my time is worked around my writing.

I live in Northumberland, England, with my husband and three cats. Whenever possible, we (not the cats) like to fit in some walking and mountain biking in the magnificent Northumberland and Kielder hills.

In the last fifteen years, I have written, for publication, the novella, Time Split and the novels: Distant Suns, Distant Suns – The Journey Home, Distant Suns – The Silexous and Islands – The Epidemic.

I strive in my writing to give the reader a rollercoaster ride of emotions and excitement, mixed in with a good dash of fear – all from the safety of their armchair.

www.ingramcontent.com/pod-product-compliance
Lightning Source LLC
Chambersburg PA
CBHW071040180925
32796CB00016B/144
* 9 7 8 1 5 4 2 7 9 3 7 7 3 *